"What happened?" Robbie demanded when the lights went out.

"Ladies and gentlemen," came a voice over the loudspeakers, "I'm sorry to announce that the power failure we're experiencing cannot be corrected at this time. We're going to have to take this train back to the station. We'll be happy to reschedule your trip or, if you prefer, refund your ticket price. On behalf of AmeriTrak, I apologize for this inconvenience and hope you have a pleasant day."

"A pleasant day?" Robbie squealed. "A pleasant *day?* We've got to get to San Diego!"

"Robbie—" hissed Josh. He gestured toward Allen, who sat behind them, holding up his right hand.

It was glowing.

The Journey of Allen Strange™

The Arrival
Invasion
Split Image
Legacy
Depth Charge

Available from MINSTREL Books

Depth Charge

Bobbi JG Weiss
&
David Cody Weiss

Published by POCKET BOOKS
New York London Toronto Sydney Tokyo Singapore

This book is a work of fiction. Names, characters, places and incidents are products of the author's imagination or are used fictitiously. Any resemblance to actual events or locales or persons, living or dead, is entirely coincidental.

A MINSTREL PAPERBACK *Original*

A Minstrel Book published by
POCKET BOOKS, a division of Simon & Schuster Inc.
1230 Avenue of the Americas, New York, NY 10020

Based on the Nickelodeon series entitled "The Journey of Allen Strange."

ISBN: 0-671-02513-9

First Minstrel Books printing July 1999

10 9 8 7 6 5 4 3 2 1

Front cover photo by Pat Hill
Back cover photo by Craig Mathew

Printed in the U.S.A.

QBP/X

To Rebecca Nystrom,
the nicest girl in all
of Santa Rosa

CHAPTER 1

THURSDAY, JUNE 24, 7:05 A.M.
THE STEVENSON HOUSE
DELPORT, CALIFORNIA

"Woohoo!"

Robbie Stevenson danced around the kitchen, happy for the first time in days. It had been a lousy week so far, and she'd been prepared to trudge through yet another boring day at school. But now everything was different.

Her father, Ken Stevenson, entered to find his sixteen-year-old daughter doing an impromptu dance around the kitchen table, shaking out a dance beat with a box of breakfast cereal. He paused in the doorway, just watching her and

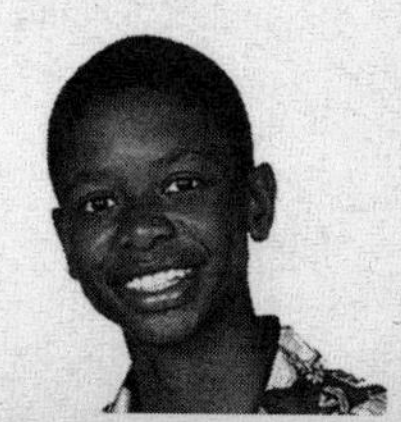

wondering if he would ever understand teenagers. He decided they were a mystery with no solution, so he merely said, "Good morning. I take it this *is* a good morning."

"It's a great morning!" Robbie crowed. "Look at the E-mail on Josh's computer!"

Josh, Robbie's younger brother, sat at the table in his usual configuration: hunkered down in his chair with his laptop computer open in front of him and a half-eaten bowl of cereal to one side. As his fingers busily tapped away at the computer keyboard, he said to his father, "Mom sent us an E-mail. She's been invited to be the guest speaker at some nursing conference at San Diego State University next weekend, and she wants to know if we can come visit while she's there."

Gail Stevenson had been separated from her husband and family for several months now. That meant that Robbie didn't get to spend much time with her mother. Visits had become a precious thing, and Robbie had no intention of missing this one. "Can we drive down, Dad?" she asked her father. "It's not far, and we've got plenty of advance notice."

Ken Stevenson squinched up his face, trying to consult his complicated work schedule by memory alone. "I don't know . . ."

"Oh, please, Dad?" whined Robbie. "We haven't seen Mom in so long, and I've never been to San Diego."

"It could be very educational," Josh added helpfully.

"Saturday," their father muttered to himself. "That's what—the third?"

"Yes," Robbie said, "and Sunday is the fourth. Mom wants us to stay long enough to watch the big Fourth of July fireworks show on San Diego Bay. It's supposed to be really spectacular."

Ken Stevenson sighed. He was a good father, and he tried awfully hard to somehow fill the role of both father and mother to his two children during his separation from Gail. But sometimes circumstances just wouldn't let him be the good guy. "I'm sorry, kids. I have to work next Saturday. The city planner's office wants me to oversee Delport's Fourth of July celebrations, remember?" Feeling like a sourpuss, he added helplessly, "Wouldn't you like to watch the fireworks here in town?"

Robbie and Josh scowled. Delport was a wonderful place to live. Right on the ocean, the town boasted clean air, white sands, an army of palm trees, pleasant weather, nice people, and Robbie's favorite distraction: surfing. But Delport couldn't

possibly offer a fireworks show to rival that of a metropolis like San Diego, let alone have a mother there as well.

Ken saw all this in Robbie's eyes. "I'm really sorry," he told her gently, "but I can't be in two places at once."

"Then why can't *we* go?" Josh suddenly suggested, pointing first to himself and then to his sister.

Robbie jumped on the possibility. "Yeah, Dad! We could ride the AmeriTrak train. It goes right to San Diego, and I promise I'll keep Josh out of trouble."

Josh's eyes narrowed to little slits. "Excuse me, but somebody needs to seriously rethink *who'll* need to keep *who* out of trouble."

"AmeriTrak," Ken Stevenson muttered, thinking it over. "Gee, I don't know . . ."

That was when Allen Strange knocked on the door.

In reality, Allen lived up in the Stevensons' attic—but Ken Stevenson didn't know that. He had no idea that Allen wasn't a neighbor at all but a space alien who'd accidentally been left behind on Earth. He had no idea that the bizarre pulsating contraption hanging like a giant cocoon in a corner of the attic was in fact a Lemorian Dream Pod in which Allen slept every night. And Ken had no idea that ever since his arrival, Allen had been the main distraction in the lives of the Stevenson children.

That was just the way Robbie and Josh wanted it.

Josh leaped to his feet and let Allen in.

"Good morning," Allen said happily, waving at his adopted human family. "Hello, Mr. Stevenson."

"Good morning, Allen," said Ken. He was used to Allen's daily visits. In fact, he sort of looked forward to them. Allen was always so cheerful that he put Ken in a good mood for work every day. "Would you like some breakfast?" he asked the boy.

Allen had been waiting for the question. It was asked every morning, and he answered the same way every morning. "Sure! Thanks!"

As he sat down, Robbie told him, "Allen, we're going San Diego next weekend to visit our mom. We're going to ride the train by ourselves. Isn't that cool?"

"Now, wait a minute," said Ken. "I haven't said you could go."

Robbie leaned toward him, pouring on all the

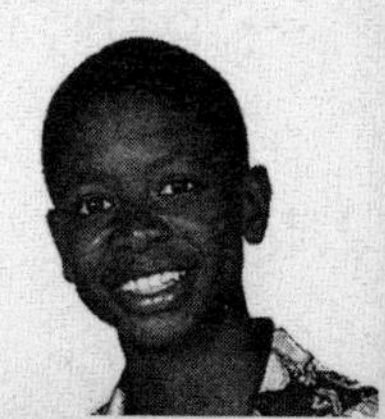

charm she could muster. "But you will, right?"

"Well . . ."

"I promise I'll baby-sit Josh anytime you ask for a whole week, and I'll do it without any complaints."

Josh didn't know whether to yell at his sister or his father. "How many times do I have to tell you guys? I don't need to be baby-sitted."

"Baby-sat," Robbie corrected him, and added to her father, "And yes, he does—right, Dad?"

Ken was no fool. He knew he was being bribed, but he also knew how much his children, especially Robbie, missed their mother. "All right," he said. "I'll go for the idea—"

The kids cheered.

"But," Ken continued in a louder voice, "only if your mother agrees, and only if she can pick you up herself at the train station. I'll call her tonight."

Robbie kissed her dad on the cheek. "She'll say yes, I know she will! Thanks, Dad!"

Ken nodded amiably, then grabbed a piece of toast and headed into the living room to get his briefcase.

Allen sat down at the table and nibbled on some dry cereal. "Wow," he said. "A train. I've never been on a train."

"They're the best," Robbie told him. "Better than stinky old buses."

"But not better than planes," Josh said. "Nothing beats flying."

Allen had to agree with that. "Especially through nebulae. They're so beautiful, particularly the purple parts."

Robbie chuckled. "Yes, well, we'll take your word for that. I doubt that our average jumbo jet is ever going to get that far."

"Too bad," Allen said sympathetically. "Maybe someday I'll be able to fly you through one. You'd love it." He munched on some more cereal. "So when do we leave?"

Robbie and Josh just looked at him. "Uh," said Josh, "*we're* not leaving."

Allen was confused. "But you just said—"

"We said that *we* were going," explained Robbie, gesturing at herself and Josh. "Allen, I'm sorry, but you'll have to stay here."

When Allen had first arrived on Earth, it had been Robbie's job to keep the curious alien out of mischief. After all, he'd known nothing about humans or their customs and had to be taught little precautions, like don't animate stone statues, don't slide *up* banisters, and don't run dental floss through your ears in public. But by now

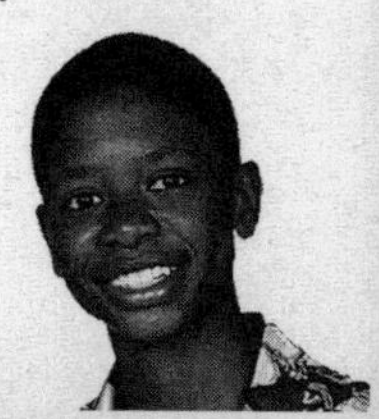

Allen had a better grasp of human behavior. Sometimes he bristled when Robbie became overprotective.

"Why can't I go with you?" he asked bluntly.

"Because . . ." Robbie floundered, "because . . . you're a minor."

"No, I'm a Xelan."

"No, I mean, you're underage. You're a kid, like us. Kids have to have permission to travel alone."

"Which is totally unfair," Josh had to add, "but it's the law."

Robbie put a hand on the alien boy's shoulder. "I'm sorry, Allen. But really, you'll be safer here. We'll only be gone over the weekend. Right, Josh?"

"Right," Josh said, trying to make Allen feel better. "You'll be able to spend some extra time in your pod and"—he started to grope—"catch up on your dreaming?"

Allen just sighed and popped a few more puffs of cereal into his mouth. Sometimes he really hated being the only alien kid on the block.

CHAPTER 2

SATURDAY, JULY 3, 7:15 A.M.
DELPORT AMERITRAK TRAIN STATION

Robbie lugged her suitcase in one hand and Josh in the other. They'd just arrived at the depot to discover that Ken's watch had been running slow. "C'mon, poky, we're late for the train," Robbie said to Josh. "Hurry up!"

Josh was struggling with his own suitcase, plus a carry-on bag containing his laptop computer and some books. "I'm coming, so just quit pulling at me!"

"Hey!" came a voice. "Doesn't the chauffeur get a good-bye hug?"

Robbie turned around to see her father stand-

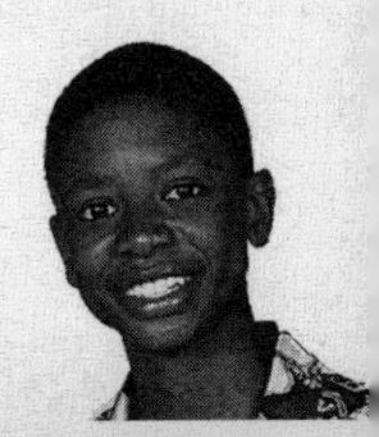

ing in the parking lot next to the car, looking forlorn. With a guilty wince, she hustled back to him, still dragging Josh after her, and gave him a hug. "Sorry, Dad. We just don't want to miss the train."

"You've got a minute or two," Ken assured her.

"Bye, Dad," said Josh. "Now, remember not to go up into the attic, okay?"

"I promise," said Ken. "I won't peek at your secret project, whatever it is. But I hope you'll show it to me when you're finished with it."

"Sure thing," Josh said, and winked at Robbie. The fact was, Josh was just using the excuse of a secret project to keep their dad from accidentally finding Allen in the attic. There was only so much the kids could explain, and lately they'd had a lot of weird adventures with Allen that had required a lot of explaining. The best tack now was to keep a low profile—or, rather, to keep *Allen's* profile low. "Now all I need to do is come up with a secret project," Josh whispered to his sister.

Robbie whispered back, "I asked Allen to take that old broken toaster to the attic and fix it so that it responds to voice commands. Will that do?"

"Perfect," Josh whispered approvingly, "as long as he can do it *quietly.*"

The train whistle gave an impatient hoot. Robbie hoisted up her suitcase again. "C'mon, Josh, we've got to go. Bye, Dad, and thanks!"

"Let me know when you get there," Ken called after them.

Once on board, Robbie and Josh chose seats and settled down. "Excellent," said Josh, gazing up the aisle, through the door, and into the snack car. "They sell Chocolate Doodle-Chews."

"Forget it," Robbie said flatly. "Dad gave us each five dollars, but it was on the condition that we buy something good for breakfast."

Josh didn't see the problem. "Chocolate Doodle-Chews *are* good for breakfast."

"I agree," came a familiar voice, "but they're not as good as spray cheese."

Robbie whirled around to find Allen sitting in the seat behind her. "Allen! How'd you get here?"

"I followed you," answered the alien.

Robbie knew that such things were not difficult for Allen to do. Because his alien body was composed mostly of light energy, he could turn his wattage down, so to speak, and become invisible at will. Still, that accomplishment didn't stop Robbie from being mad at him. "Allen, I thought I told you not to come," she said, grate-

ful that nobody else on the train had noticed the alien's sudden appearance. Most people were busy stowing their luggage in the overhead bins or, if they were already settled, reading the latest issue of the AmeriTrak onboard magazine.

"Robbie, you said I needed *permission* to come," Allen said calmly. "Well, I got permission."

Josh snorted, realizing what their intergalactic friend must have done. "You asked Manfred, didn't you?"

Nodding proudly, Allen took a slip of paper from his shirt pocket and handed it to Robbie. "I had him write me a note and everything, just like for school."

Robbie read the paper. Sure enough, it was a permission slip for Allen to ride an AmeriTrak train alone, but the writing was so sloppy she could hardly make it out. Manfred wasn't very good at penmanship—he was just a mannequin, after all. Ever since the day Allen had seen him in a store window and energized him with light power, Manfred the mannequin had become Allen's father-away-from-home. He could do almost anything a real person could do, if he was energized enough. When Allen didn't need him, Manfred quietly stood in a corner of the attic, stiff as plastic . . . which was exactly what he was made of.

Robbie's anger melted away, as it always did when Allen outsmarted her. "Okay, you got permission," she conceded, "but on a train, you also need a ticket. Do you have one?"

"No," answered Allen simply.

Josh sighed. "Great. We're in for it when the conductor comes around."

Confused now, Allen pointed out, "Why would I want to get a ticket? Isn't that a bad thing?"

"When a cop gives you one, yes," Robbie explained. "But you have to have a ticket to ride on a train or a plane or a bus. Get it?"

"Ohhhh." Now Allen understood. However, he was a Xelan kid who'd managed to travel across the entire universe without any kind of ticket at all. It certainly couldn't be too hard to obtain one for a little train ride on Earth. "So how do I get one?" he asked.

"He can buy one from the conductor, can't he?" Josh asked his sister.

Without a word, Robbie held up her five-dollar bill. Even combined with Josh's money, it would hardly equal the price of a ticket.

Josh pursed his lips. "We're in trouble."

The train jerked once, then slowly began to

move. Robbie turned to see the conductor carefully shut the door, sealing all passengers inside. Through the window she watched the depot grounds slide past, followed by downtown Delport, which slipped by faster and faster as the train gained speed. Then the suburbs disappeared behind them, leaving nothing but open land ahead, with the ocean on the right and marshes on the left. San Diego lay far ahead, due south . . . and Allen sat behind her, without a ticket.

"What are we going to do?" Josh asked. "The conductor will start checking tickets any minute."

Robbie just sat there as the train gently rocked on the rails, every now and then *clackity-clacking* over a particularly rough piece of track. "I don't know" was all she could think of to say.

That's when the lights went out.

Everybody in the train car jumped in surprise, but nobody panicked. Bright sunlight was still streaming in through the windows on the east, so there was plenty of light to see by. "What happened?" Robbie demanded. She didn't know who might have an answer, but the question had to be spoken aloud.

"Ladies and gentlemen, may I have your attention, please?" came a voice over the loudspeakers. As the train slowly ground to a halt, the voice continued, "We seem to have a hiccup in the onboard electrical system. Please stay in your seats. We should have the problem solved in a few minutes. Thank you for your patience."

"Thank goodness," Robbie sighed. "If we can't get to San Diego . . ." She didn't finish the sentence. If they couldn't go to San Diego, she wouldn't get to see her mother. On the other hand, going to San Diego would surely mean trouble for Allen. Robbie thought about how much she wanted to see her mom, then about how much she wanted to protect Allen. Soon she didn't know which outcome to wish for.

Fortunately, fate made up her mind for her. "Ladies and gentlemen," came the voice over the speakers again, "I'm sorry to announce that the power failure we're experiencing cannot be corrected at this time. We're going to have to take this train back to the station. We'll be happy to reschedule your trip or, if you prefer, refund your ticket price. On behalf of AmeriTrak, I apologize for this inconvenience and hope you have a pleasant day."

"A pleasant day?" Robbie squealed. *"A pleasant day?* We've got to get to San Diego!"

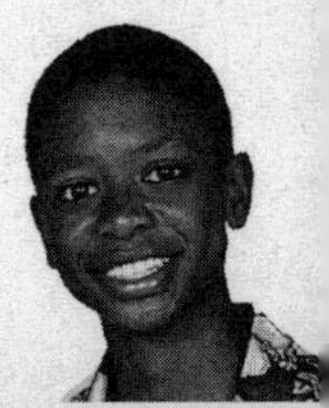

"Robbie," hissed Josh, "you're forgetting something."

"And what might that be?" Robbie snapped, in no mood for one of Josh's pranks.

But this was no prank. Josh gestured toward Allen, who sat behind them, holding up his right hand.

It was glowing.

CHAPTER 3

7:28 A.M.
AMERITRAK TRAIN NO. 446
EN ROUTE TO SAN DIEGO

Before Robbie could say a word, Allen and Josh were up out of their seats and heading for the back of the train. Robbie followed them. "Allen, wait. You're not thinking what I think you're thinking, are you?"

"Yup, he's thinking it," Josh answered for the Xelan.

"This must be it." Allen tapped his finger against a big metal box attached to the back wall of the train car. "It's a circuit box, but it's locked. That shouldn't be a problem, though." He placed

his hand flat against the lid of the box and closed his eyes.

Robbie slapped her hand over his. "Wait, Allen. Are you sure you can do this without, you know, blowing up the train?" She'd seen him successfully use his light energy to energize Josh's goofy gadgets, her father's broken-down sports car, and even Manfred the mannequin. However, being only a Xelan kid, Allen sometimes misjudged his power flow and ended up blowing out windows and flash-frying electrical circuits, not to mention making her hair all frizzy.

Allen opened his eyes and blinked at her. "Do trains blow up easily?"

"All the time," Josh said, "especially in action movies."

"Then I'll be careful," Allen promised.

That sounded good enough for Robbie, under the circumstances. "Okay, but we can't let the passengers see the light." She turned to Josh. "You go distract them."

"Me?" said Josh. "Why me? Why not you?"

"Because I'm bigger so I have to hide Allen. Go on."

Disgusted at being ordered around, Josh returned to his seat. But by the time he got there, he'd come up with a plan. "Okay, maybe it's better I do the distracting," he muttered to himself. "Robbie could never think of a cool plan like this."

He glanced back to find his sister casually standing in front of Allen, trying to hide him with her slim body as best she could. He nodded once to her, as a signal, then turned back to face the window by his seat. "Hey, everybody, look outside!" he suddenly bellowed. "That hang glider is about to crash into us!"

A swell of alarmed voices filled the train car, and the passengers automatically looked out their windows. At that moment Allen phased into his light form and infused the circuit box with blue-white energy that flowed from the palm of his hand.

The rear end of the car blazed with light, but nobody noticed. Nor did anyone notice when all the lights in the train flickered back on. People still had their faces pressed to the windows, trying to see the alleged hang glider outside. "What the heck are you talking about, kid?" a burly man finally said, clearly disappointed. "I don't see no hang glider."

His mission accomplished, Josh gave a noncommittal shrug. "He must have caught an

updraft. Talk about good luck. Hey, the lights are back on!"

Now everybody looked at the light fixtures to find them blazing happily away. Murmurs of relief filled the car, and the loudspeaker crackled to life. "Ladies and gentlemen, may I have your attention, please? It seems that we've managed to correct the electrical problem after all. We'll be under way in just a few minutes."

Everybody clapped while Robbie and Allen casually walked back to their seats. When he reached his, Allen didn't so much sit down as collapse into it. "You okay?" Robbie asked him, concerned.

"Yeah," he answered tiredly. "It just took a little out of me, that's all. This is a pretty big train."

Robbie pushed her five-dollar bill into Josh's hand. "Go buy him something to eat, to help him get his strength back," she said. "And get me a couple of doughnuts while you're at it."

"What am I, your personal slave?" Josh grumbled. "And what's with you getting doughnuts when I can't get Chocolate Doodle-Chews?"

Robbie realized he was right. "Josh, I'm sorry. Go get whatever you want. You've earned it."

"Darned right I have," Josh said and, snatching

her five, headed down the aisle to the snack car.

"Do you think they sell spray cheese?" asked Allen softly, slumped in his seat. Cheese in a can, especially bacon-cheddar flavor, was Allen's favorite Earth food.

"I doubt it," Robbie answered with a chuckle. "But you know what, Allen? I think you just earned a ride to San Diego."

Allen smiled weakly. "Great. But what do I do when the conductor comes by?"

She smiled back. "You'll think of something."

As it turned out, Allen had to think of something real fast. The conductor entered the car and began to take tickets. Grateful that there weren't many passengers in their car, Allen called on his alien shape-shifting talents and silently phased *into* his seat, sinking down until the molecules of his body mingled perfectly with the molecules of the seat. The conductor took the two tickets that Robbie held out—one for her and one for Josh—and after he'd punched the tickets and left, Allen silently phased his body back to solidity.

"That was perfect," Robbie congratulated him. Then she noticed that his face had gone pale. "Allen, you sure you're okay?"

Exhausted but grinning, Allen handed her a quarter and two dimes that he'd found between

the seat cushions. "I'll be fine. Don't worry. I just need—"

"A peanut butter sandwich," said Josh, arriving with a handful of packaged foods. "I got you that and some milk, Allen. Lots of protein."

"Thanks," Allen said, and eagerly started eating.

"Here's two chocolate doughnuts with rainbow sprinkles for you," Josh continued, passing them over to Robbie. "And for me"—he happily shook the box—"a jumbo-size box of Chocolate Doodle-Chews. It's chow time!"

Twenty minutes later and fifty miles farther down the tracks, Allen's strength was restored to normal. Since he'd never been on a train before, Robbie and Josh invited him on a tour. "There isn't really anyplace special to go," Robbie admitted as they wandered from car to car, squeezing through the narrow aisles, trying not to step on people's toes, and pausing to avoid the toddlers who now and again managed to wander away from their parents. "This is just a commuter train, so it's not very big."

"I think it's plenty big," Allen said, remembering the amount of energy it had taken to restore the train's electricity.

"You know what kind of trains are cool?" said

Josh as they headed back to their own car. "Sleeper trains. They have special rooms on top that have nothing but big windows so you can watch the scenery go by, and they have whole restaurant cars and playrooms and TVs and all sorts of stuff. The chairs are a lot more comfortable, too."

"We took one to Arizona once," Robbie explained to Allen. "Mom and Dad promised to take us to see the Grand Canyon, but they didn't want to drive. I liked the train ride almost as much as the Grand Canyon itself."

"The Grand Canyon?" Allen asked. "What's that?"

"A big hole in the ground, carved by a river," Josh said. "It's awesome."

"Humans take train rides just to see a hole in the ground?" Allen shook his head. "Strange culture."

"Oh, you think so?" asked Josh. "Okay, so where do Xelans go to sightsee?"

Allen thought about it as he moved aside, allowing a woman carrying a baby to go by. "When I was little, my Nurturers took me to see the Giant Time Whorls of Gamdya. They say that if you walk too close to the biggest ones, you could get stuck in the same moment of time for eternity."

"They can just suck you up into a time loop?" Josh asked. "Cool!"

"Oh, right, cool," said Robbie. "I'd like to see you get stuck washing your face over and over and over for all time."

The very idea made Josh twitch. Taking a bath every night was chore enough. The concept of washing for eternity was positively nauseating. "Yeah, well," he retorted, "if *you* got stuck in one while you were on the phone with one of your gabby girlfriends, I bet you'd still be yakking even after eternity ran out."

Robbie drew in a breath, ready to lob an equally scathing insult at her brother, when the voice of the conductor came over the speakers. "Ladies and gentlemen, our next stop is San Diego. San Diego is our next stop."

"That's us!" Robbie hurried the rest of the way to their seats and took her suitcase down from the overhead luggage locker. Then she hauled down Josh's smaller suitcase and his computer bag.

Allen stared at them. "Should I have brought bags also?"

"That depends," Robbie said. "Did you have anything you needed to bring on the trip?"

Allen thought about it. "No," he concluded.

"Then you didn't need a bag," Josh told him. "C'mon, let's wait by the door."

They hurried to the exit door. The sound of the wheels on the tracks just beneath the floor were much louder here, and Allen seemed to enjoy it, clicking and humming to himself in time with the clacking wheels. Robbie wondered if he was singing some kind of Xelan song to the rhythm of the train.

Through the window the three kids watched the city of San Diego approach. The cozy seaside community of Pacific Beach gave way to a sprawling hotel and resort complex on tranquil Mission Bay. Fancy hotels and restaurants lined the shore, and Robbie watched tourists and locals alike travel across the beautiful blue water on speedboats and sailboats while swimmers splashed and floated nearer the shore. She could even spot picnickers cooking outdoor feasts in the big fire pits that dotted the sandy beach. In the distance, on the south shore of Mission Bay, lay the sprawling expanse of the famous ocean theme park called Sea World.

The train crossed a bridge spanning a wide channel, after which the famous San Diego Sports Arena passed by to the west while historic Old Town glided by to the east. Minutes later the

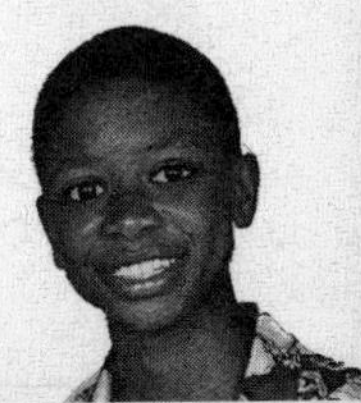

train squeaked to a gentle stop at the depot downtown. The conductor opened the door, positioned a set of steps in place, and Robbie, Josh, and Allen scrambled out.

Allen stood on the tarmac at the station, sniffing the air and studying the horizon. San Diego Bay lay to the west, while the eastern view was now dominated by a hillside covered with quaint stucco houses, rows of business buildings, and lots of palm trees. "Nice," he concluded.

Robbie checked her watch. "We'd better hustle to the harbor. Mom got us those tour tickets, and since the train was late, we've barely got enough time to get there."

"Tour?" Allen asked.

"Yeah, of the whole harbor," said Josh. "Mom can't come pick us up for another hour, and she didn't want us to get bored waiting at the station. You'll need a ticket too, but I think we've got enough money to spring for it. C'mon."

The harbor wasn't far away, so the three kids walked there after Robbie and Josh stowed their suitcases in lockers at the station. When Allen realized he was about to ride in a boat on the water, he began to run. "My life force!" he crowed, referring to the water. "I've never *ridden* on it before. I don't want to miss this!"

Laughing, Robbie and Josh ran after him. A short while later, Allen Strange, alien stowaway from the planet Xela, stepped aboard a boat for the first time.

CHAPTER 4

10:00 A.M.
ABOARD A HARBOR TOUR BOAT
SAN DIEGO BAY

"Welcome to the San Diego Harbor tour," said the guide, a tall brunette with sparkling blue eyes. She stood on a little platform with a microphone in her hand. "My name is Lacey, and I'll be pointing out some of the sights as we cover twelve miles of the bay in approximately one hour."

"Hi, Lacey!" cheered a bunch of Hawaiian-shirted tourists to Robbie's left. She, Josh, and Allen stood with a crowd of sightseers on the deck of one of seven boats designed specifically for touring San Diego Bay. As the boat eased away from its dock, the chugging of its engines made the deck shudder beneath their feet.

Lacey was chuckling into her microphone. "Ah, a good crowd, I see. Okay, let's get under way." With an audible clunk, the engines shifted gear and the boat chugged faster.

Robbie breathed in the crisp ocean air. She never got tired of the ocean. Sometimes she wondered what it would be like to live inland, but the very thought made her jittery. She'd decided long ago that life without surfing would be pointless. Judging by all the sun-bleached blondes she'd seen around, lots of other people felt as she did.

Lacey, too, had the tan of a beach lover. "San Diego Bay covers twenty-two square miles," she was saying into her microphone. "It's a natural deepwater harbor whose entrance is protected by two peninsulas—Coronado to the east and Point Loma to the west. The bay serves as the headquarters for the Eleventh U.S. Naval District, as well as a base of operations for the army, marines, and coast guard. It's also home to commercial fishing fleets. The Thirty-second Street Naval Station, south of here, was once the site of one of California's biggest tuna fisheries." She gestured

back to the dock they were leaving. "The first site of interest was right next to us when you boarded—the *Star of India.* You can see her a little better as we pull away."

Robbie had already noticed the beautiful old sailing vessel docked next to the touring facility. It was hard not to notice—the *Star of India* loomed over the boardwalk like a grand ghost from the past, her huge masts reaching high up into the sky, the wood of her rails polished so that they gleamed in the sunlight. "She's a barkentine," their guide explained, "one of the oldest iron sailing ships in the world. She's been completely restored and functions mainly as a maritime museum these days, but she's still fully functional and sails once or twice a year under the care of a specially trained crew."

Lacey next pointed out the Cruise Ship Terminal where the famous *Pacific Princess* took on passengers, and the Downtown marina where the former America's Cup boat *Stars and Stripes* was docked.

The tour boat chugged its way past North Island Naval Air Station. Robbie tried to listen to Lacey's ongoing commentary, but she had to keep an eye on Josh, who rarely stayed in the same spot for more than two seconds. He kept dashing from rail to rail, trying to see everything at once. Naturally Allen followed him, so naturally Robbie had to follow them both.

"Navy ships come and go every day," Lacey explained at one point. "Some of you may have heard a peculiar sound out here—five blasts of a ship's horn. That's a warning signal to smaller boats whose owners may not know that all ships larger than sixty-five feet have the right-of-way in the bay. This is because larger ships have less maneuverability. As you can guess, the bay can get pretty busy sometimes."

Next, Lacey pointed out the lines of steel gray navy ships docked at North Island, including the USS *Constellation,* an enormous aircraft carrier. On the opposite shore she pointed out the San Diego Naval Training Station, where the famous USS *Neversail* was located. Robbie had heard about the *Neversail,* a mock ship set in concrete where boot camp trainees learned the ways of the sea before ever going out onto the water. The old boot camp was gone now, but near it were the ASW—Anti-Submarine War Base—and the San Diego Yacht Club. Farther south was Point Loma, where NOSC—the Naval Operations Surveillance Command—was located. "Aside from NOSC, it's been rumored that the Point is

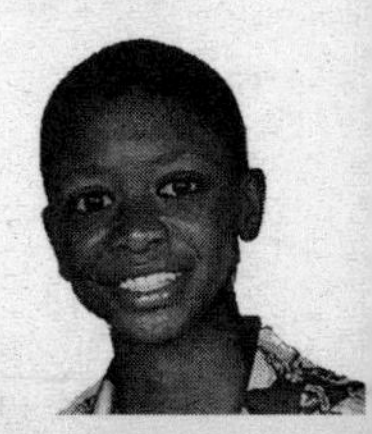

completely honeycombed with secret naval surveillance installations," Lacey said. "If so, then they've taken great care not to disturb the veterans who rest in the beautiful national cemetery."

"Cemetery," Josh scoffed. "That's just a cover. I bet there's more secret stuff going on inside the Point than anybody could guess. They probably watch everything that happens all over the world. I bet they've even got a secret UFO tracking station!"

Robbie just snorted. "Dream on, Josh."

Josh turned to Allen. "What do you think, Allen?"

"I think that anything is possible," said Allen, "especially when it comes to government conspiracies."

Josh beamed at Robbie. "See? I've trained him well."

"You've brainwashed him, you mean," said Robbie. "That's all I need—a paranoid little brother *and* a paranoid alien."

The tour boat made its way south, and Robbie watched the majestic Coronado Bridge loom overhead. "The bridge links downtown San Diego with Coronado Island," Lacey said. "Some of you visitors may want to ride the ferry from Broadway Pier near the convention center over to the Ferry Landing Marketplace on the island. One of Coronado's biggest attractions, of course, is the Hotel del Coronado, a national historic landmark. Built in 1888 and renovated in 1997, it has over six hundred rooms and is the largest oceanfront resort on the entire West Coast."

Robbie heard none of this last part. She was searching for Josh, who'd disappeared with Allen. Again. Weaving her way among the gawking tourists, she finally found the boys at the bow of the ship. Allen was leaning over the rail, grinning like a happy kid as the waves splashed up against the prow. "I love this!" he said over the sound of wind and waves. "I'm riding on my life force!" Whenever spray hit his face, he giggled.

Robbie couldn't help but giggle, too. Allen's enthusiasm was infectious. "Just be careful," she warned him. "Your life force is very cold and deep."

"Coronado Island isn't really an island," came Lacey's voice over the ship's loudspeaker. "The thin strip of beach that protects the west side of San Diego Bay is actually man-made and is known as the Silver Strand. The Strand is mined, so that if the northern access to the bay is ever cut off, the strand can be blown away to create access to navy and shipping facilities."

"Boy, a blast like that would be something to see," Josh said. "There'd be sand everywhere!"

"I doubt it," Robbie said, though she had no actual facts to back up her doubt. It was just her duty to contradict any outrageous comments Josh made. She thought of it as her job as big sister. "Besides," she said, "we'd have to be at war or something for them to blow up a whole—"

She never finished her sentence. At that moment a speedboat roared past, and as Robbie and Josh watched, foaming water slapped up the prow and hit Allen right in the face, completely drenching him. He was so startled that, for just an instant, he shifted into his energy body and let out a whoop of delighted surprise.

Robbie saw him start to glow. "Allen!" she cried out in alarm.

Allen quickly regained his human form, but now he stood as still as a statue, an expression of bafflement on his face. "I just felt something . . . strange," he said.

CHAPTER 5

10:22 A.M.
ABOARD THE TOUR BOAT

"Strange how?" Robbie pressed the alien.

As cold seawater dripped from his body, Allen struggled to unscramble his jumbled thoughts. "I'm not sure. While in my light form, I sensed an energy signal that seemed . . . familiar."

The way Allen spoke made Josh nervous. "Familiar how?"

"It was close to the detonation frequency that the Trykloids use for their *jbypidoch.*"

"What's a . . . jabippydock?" Robbie said, trying and failing miserably to repeat the word.

Normally Allen would have been amused by

such an awkward mispronunciation, but this wasn't a word to be laughed at. He wiped water from his face with his sleeve and explained ominously, "It's a horrible weapon with incredible destructive power. You see, Trykloids don't possess Xelan light powers, so long ago they created a power for themselves using technology. You could say that a *jbypidoch* is a kind of bomb, but a bomb without form, composed of pure potential *dark* energy. When the correct signal is aimed at the potential source, the energy takes form and explodes." The mere thought of such a weapon made Allen's face grow pale. "I didn't sense the exact *jbypidoch* detonation signal, but it was awfully close. If your military is experimenting with the same power principles discovered by the Trykloids, your planet is in great danger. A *jbypidoch* is more destructive than humans could possibly imagine."

Josh turned to his sister. "This could be enough to make me panic. What about you?"

"Don't panic just yet," Robbie whispered, and without warning, she let loose a big, overblown laugh. "Wow, that was some wave, Allen!" she said loudly. "You're all wet!"

Josh and Allen looked at her like some kind of nut, then realized that she was trying to cover for them. Allen's accidental shift to his light body had caught everybody's attention, and the other tourists were eyeing them. No doubt they were wondering what three kids were doing clustered together, talking in hushed voices after such a strange light had flashed out of nowhere.

Josh forced himself to laugh, too. "That was a good trick, Allen," he said loud enough for everybody to hear. Then he grasped the alien's arm. "C'mon, let's get you dried off."

Robbie took Allen's other arm, and they led him down a flight of stairs to the lower deck, where the snack bar and lounge were located. Since most of the tourists wanted to be outside to watch the sights, the three teens were alone now except for the snack bar attendant.

Robbie and Josh led Allen to a table in the corner. "Allen, you can't shift into your light body any time you feel like it," she whispered sternly, handing him a wad of napkins so he could dry himself off. "One of these days the wrong people will see you, and then we'll all be in trouble."

"It was an accident. I'm sorry," Allen said, mopping his face with the napkins. "That signal was so strong—"

Josh interrupted him. "Robbie, what if he's

right? What if the signal he sensed really was a jabiddybock—"

"Jbypidoch," Allen corrected him.

"Whatever," said Josh. "You presume he imagined it. What if he didn't?"

"Oh, c'mon, Josh," said Robbie. "Do you really believe that our scientists have discovered the same weapon that the Trykloids invented? We can hardly get a rocket into space, let alone create potential energy bombs." She turned to Allen apologetically. "Allen, whatever you sensed, I'm sure it wasn't a jibobbyduck."

"Jbypidoch," Allen corrected her.

"Whatever. You heard what the tour guide said—there are naval installations all over San Diego Bay. You probably just sensed a radio signal."

Josh adamantly shook his head. "I say we let Allen double-check the phenomenon. The survival of Earth may hang in the balance!"

Allen set down the wad of now wet napkins and pinned Robbie with one of his sincere stares, the kind that she just couldn't say no to. "He's right, Robbie. This could be important."

Robbie held her hands up in surrender. "Okay. Fine. Go save planet Earth. But don't let anybody see you."

"Check!" Josh glanced around furtively, then stood up. "We'll head for the bathroom," he whispered to Allen. "You can shift into your light form there and nobody will see."

"While you're in there, finish drying off," Robbie said.

Allen nodded, and the two boys hurried away. Robbie continued to sit where she was, compulsively tapping her foot. She wasn't sure if the foot-tapping was the result of nervousness or excitement—being with Allen could often be a double-edged sword. Sure, she loved the adventure that he brought into her life, and she valued his friendship more than she ever would have dreamed. But sometimes her nerves couldn't stand the strain of worrying about him and the bizarre things that always seemed to happen around him. The very thought that there could be a real jadippydack, or whatever it was, on Earth was a little freaky. She hoped he was wrong about it.

When the boys returned, Josh looked disappointed and Allen looked confused.

"I take it that you didn't sense the signal this time," Robbie said, not without some satisfaction.

"Correct," Allen admitted. "I don't understand it."

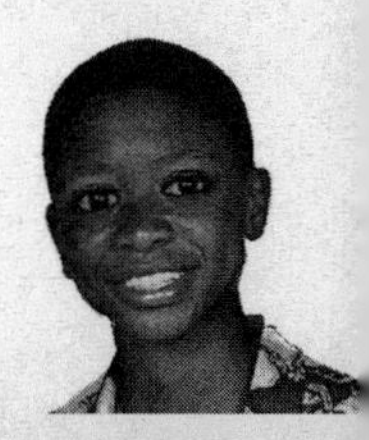

"It's obviously a secret government signal," said Josh. "Probably intermittent and scrambled. I think we ought to investigate."

"I think you're out of your mind." Robbie stood up. "Enough with government conspiracies. Let's finish the tour."

They stepped back out onto the deck to discover that the tour was over. The boat was slowly gliding back to its berth, and all the other passengers were lining up to disembark. "Great. We missed half of it," Robbie complained.

"Tell you what," Josh offered. "I'll look up San Diego Bay on the Internet tonight and download all the information you could ever possibly want—more than the tour guide could tell you, I bet."

Robbie appreciated the offer, but reading statistics off a computer screen wasn't quite the same as standing on the prow of a boat, listening to stories while the crisp sea wind blew through your hair. "Thanks, Josh, but no thanks."

"Suit yourself," Josh said.

To Robbie's delight, they returned to the train station just in time to see Gail Stevenson getting out of a car that sat idling in the loading zone. "Mom!" Robbie burst into a run and threw herself into her mother's arms.

Gail stumbled back a bit, surprised by the enthusiasm of her daughter's greeting. "Gee, has it really been that long?" she asked, bemused.

"Too long," said Robbie. "How are you? You look good."

Indeed, her mother looked very good. Since she'd been attending a conference all morning, she was dressed in a tailored business suit—something Robbie rarely saw her sports-minded mother wear. "Yup," Gail said, "I had to blend in with the office types." She waved. "Josh! Over here!"

Robbie turned to find Josh approaching more slowly. After all, it wasn't cool for an eleven-year-old boy to run into his mother's arms. Robbie also noticed that Allen had disappeared—Josh had probably lagged behind to cover for him. "Hi, Mom," Josh said when he reached her. "The harbor tour was great. Thanks for getting us tickets."

"You're welcome. I'm glad you liked it." Gail turned to face the car she'd arrived in, and indicated a young woman who was now standing by the driver's side. Only then did Robbie register that her mother had gotten out on the passenger side. "Kids, this is Pamela Burkes, an old college buddy of mine."

Pamela, a tall, lithe brunette, cast a mock-angry glare at her friend. "Old?" she said. "Who are you calling old?"

Gail laughed. "Oops. Sorry. Kids, this is Pamela Burkes, an incredibly young friend from my old college days. How's that?"

Pamela laughed too. "Perfect. Hi, Robbie. Hi, Josh. Your mother's told me a lot about you two."

"Uh-oh," Robbie and Josh said in unison.

"Don't worry, it was all bad," Pamela added gaily.

Robbie smiled. She liked Pamela already. Anybody who made jokes about her mom was going to be fun.

Gail glanced at her watch. "Robbie, Josh, you'd better get your suitcases. We're on a tight schedule."

The kids retrieved their gear from the locker, then piled it into the trunk of the car. Robbie climbed into the back seat with Josh, hoping that Allen was somewhere aboard as Pamela revved the engine.

"Cool sound system," Josh said, leaning forward between the two front seats to admire the radio–CD player. "Got any good radio stations around here?"

Pamela punched at the controls. "Of course.

There's KDAY—that's local—and then there's XROK from across the border, and then—"

Static blared from the speakers.

"Didn't that happen yesterday when you picked me up?" asked Gail.

Pamela nodded. "I keep forgetting—every time I drive near the water here, the radio goes fritzy. Must be a power pole or something. I'll try it again later." She punched the radio off and pulled the car onto the road, heading for the long, graceful bridge that Robbie remembered from the harbor tour.

"That's the Coronado Bay Bridge, right?" she said.

"Yes, it is," said Gail, impressed. "Pam has a house out on Coronado Island. We'll be staying there with her and her daughter, Vonda, who's just about your age, by the way."

"A year older," Pamela corrected. "Heaven forbid if you accidentally push her back a year. She's so anxious to reach eighteen she'll probably explode when she finally gets there."

Robbie snickered, but she understood all too well the lure of legal adulthood. Eighteen promised to be a truly amazing age for her, too . . . in two years. "So how did you and my mom meet?" she asked.

"We were dorm roommates," Pamela replied. "Freshman year—boy, was that ever an adventure. I still remember how much your mother snored. She was like a bear. I could never get any sleep."

"I did not snore like a bear," Gail countered hotly. "On the other hand, I distinctly remember those awful canned sardines you liked to eat. Jeez, they stunk up the whole room."

"Ewww," Josh said at the mere thought.

"Smelly little fish are good for you," was all Pamela would say.

Gail huffed. "Well, in any case, you could say that PeeBee and I were the scourge of the pre-med department."

Josh cast an inquiring gaze at Pamela. "PeeBee?" he asked.

"My initials," she explained. "Gail called me PeeBee, and I called her Dozer."

That made Robbie laugh. "Why? Did my mom fall asleep in class a lot?" She poked her mother's shoulder. "See, I told you it was hereditary."

Pamela grinned in amusement. "No, Dozer is short for 'bulldozer.' I was convinced that your mom made it through college because she just squared her shoulders and bulldozed her way through."

"There you go again," Gail protested, "making up stories about me."

"You know it's true," retorted Pamela. "Anybody who got in your way ended up flat on the road. Admit it."

Robbie and Josh exchanged knowing looks with a shared, "Ahh," of understanding. They'd seen their mother in bulldozer mode many times.

"Oh, don't listen to her," Gail said. "I was just highly motivated. So was Pam. She graduated with honors, became a nurse, and is now a nurse practitioner on staff at Mercy Hospital."

"And I love it," Pamela said.

Robbie finally had to ask a question that had been on her mind ever since her mother arrived. "If both of you are busy at the conference this weekend, when will we have time to visit? Now?" she added hopefully.

"I wish we could," Gail answered, "but Pam and I have to get back to the conference. We'll drop you off at Pamela's house, and Vonda will show you around town. She's got a driver's license and a car."

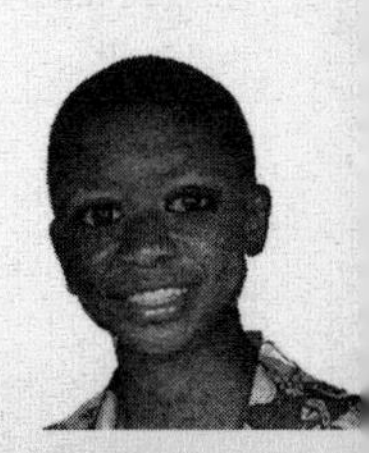

"Lucky," Josh commented.

"We can visit tonight, and then tomorrow night we'll all go out to Glorietta Bay in Pam's boat to watch the fireworks."

Robbie approved of the schedule, but there was just one little hitch: what about Allen? He'd wanted to ride on the train, but now what was he going to do? He couldn't stay hidden through the entire weekend . . . could he?

Robbie glanced around the car, wondering where he was. She tried not to gasp when she glanced out her window—Allen's light-body head was sticking out of the trunk! Like a dog with its head out a car window—except there was no window—Allen was sticking his head out of the car itself, enjoying the view as it whizzed by.

And what a view it was. The Coronado Bay Bridge was high enough that she could see the entire city, all the way north to La Jolla and all the way south to Mexico. It took Robbie's breath away.

The car touched down onto the soil of Coronado Island, and Pamela drove them into a cozy residential area. They finally stopped in front of a brown two-story house with a stone fence and two enormous palm trees.

A young girl who must have been Vonda burst out the front door and trotted down the stairs leading from the porch to the perfectly manicured lawn. "Mom!" she bawled. "What's the idea of taking my credit card?"

Robbie and Josh looked at each other as Gail muttered quietly, "Oh, dear . . ."

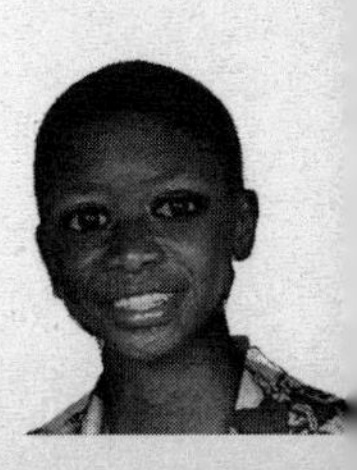

CHAPTER 6

11:58 A.M.
THE BURKES' HOUSE
CORONADO ISLAND

The car stopped and Pamela got out. "Vonda honey, the Stevensons are here."

"Hi!" Vonda said cheerfully to her guests. Then her face reverted to a frown as she said to her mother, "Now, what about my credit card?"

Pamela discreetly took her daughter aside as Robbie, Josh, and Gail got out of the car. "Is she always like that?" Robbie asked quietly.

Gail shook her head. "Vonda's a very nice girl, but sometimes she gets a little . . . intense. You two know better than to say anything, right?"

"Of course, Mom," Robbie assured her.

As Gail moved away, Josh muttered to his sister, "Man, she's got a license, a car, *and* her own credit card?"

"I wish I was intense," Robbie muttered back.

They joined the others. Now Vonda was all smiles. "Sorry about that," she apologized to them. "I thought I'd lost my card, and, well, I kind of panicked. You know how it is."

"Sure," Robbie said, not knowing how it was at all. "I'm Robbie. Hi."

"And I'm Josh."

"I'm Vondalee Antoinette, but just call me Vonda." In a crisp, businesslike way, Vonda shook Robbie's hand, then Josh's.

Josh couldn't resist. "Sorry," he said, "but we don't have any business cards with us today."

Robbie poked him as Gail asked Vonda, "Are you sure you don't mind being tour guide this afternoon?"

"Not at all, Mrs. Stevenson. It'll be fun. C'mon, you guys!" Vonda grabbed Robbie's suitcase and headed into the house.

Despite its lush surroundings, the Burkes' house wasn't as big as Robbie had thought. She was surprised to discover that there was no spare room for guests. She would be sharing Vonda's

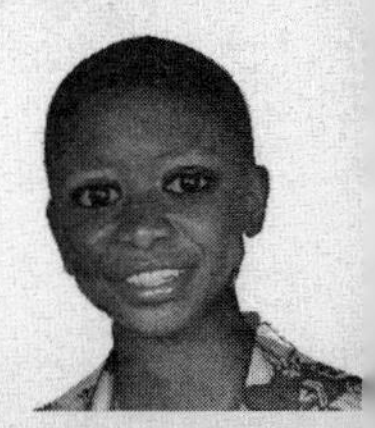

room, Josh was going to sleep on the couch in the den, and Gail would share Pamela's room.

After they'd had a chance to freshen up, Pamela said, "All right, troops, Gail and I have to go now. We'll be back around six or six-thirty, okay?"

"Okay," Vonda answered. "We'll be back by then, too."

As much as she wanted to see her mother, Robbie couldn't help but be excited about spending the day with Vonda. It wasn't often that she had a chance to explore a whole city without adults around. "So where are we off to?"

"How about the harbor?" Josh suggested.

Robbie gave him a funny look. "We were just there."

"Well, yeah," Josh admitted, then grabbed her arm. "Can I have a word with you, please? Excuse us, Vonda."

Pulling Robbie into the family room, Josh said, "What about Allen? What about that signal? We can't just wander around all day without looking into it."

"Josh, the last time Allen tried, he didn't even sense the signal."

"True," came a voice, "but like Josh, I'm eager to try again."

Robbie whirled around to find Allen standing right behind her. "Stop doing that!" she blurted, then lowered her voice. "Just be sure Vonda doesn't see you."

"She won't." Allen checked out the room, commenting, "Nice place."

Josh returned to the original topic. "What if Allen and I investigate while you and Vonda see the sights?"

"No way," said Robbie. "We have to stay together. If anything happened to you, Mom would kill me. Look, will you do me a favor and quit feeding Allen's imagination? Or, Allen, quit feeding Josh's imagination. Whichever it is, okay? Today is not the day to go bomb hunting. Period." She left the room before Josh or Allen could say another word.

"Brother-sister argument?" Vonda asked her when she emerged.

"Sort of. You know little brothers."

Vonda simply pursed her lips as if the very idea of younger boys put a bad taste in her mouth. "I'm glad I'm an only child."

They spent the next few minutes locking the house up, and then the kids headed for Vonda's car. "A convertible!" Josh cried when he saw the sleek cherry-red car. "It's all yours?"

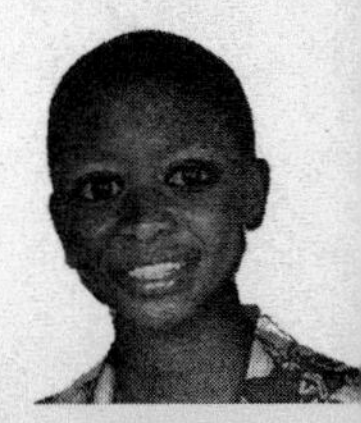

Lovingly, Vonda brushed a speck of dust from the hood. "Yeah, it's my dad's old car. He gave it to me when he and my mom split up—a good-bye present, I guess."

Stung by the news, Robbie wanted to say something, just a little word of sympathy. After all, she sort of knew how Vonda felt. But she didn't get a chance. Vonda leaped over the door and right into the driver's seat. "So get in and let's go!" Robbie and Josh followed suit, Robbie in the passenger seat and Josh in the back. "I know the perfect place to take you guys. It's called Balboa Park. I consider it the cultural center of the city."

Vonda drove them back over the Coronado Bay Bridge, onto the freeway, and soon they were driving along a road lined with tall eucalyptus trees. Robbie had never seen so many eucalyptus trees in her life. "Koala bears can only eat eucalyptus leaves. Did you know that?" said Vonda.

Actually, Robbie did. "I had to write a paper on Australia last year at school," she explained.

"Oh." Vonda searched her memory for another factual tidbit. "Well, my mom told me that most of the buildings in Balboa Park were built back in the early 1900s for a big exposition celebrating the building of the Panama Canal. Part of the 163 freeway was actually a huge artificial lake they built just for the expo. Isn't that amazing? But now only a few of the buildings in the park and at the zoo are left."

One word caught Josh's attention. "Zoo?"

"Yeah, you know—where they keep wild animals?" Robbie teased.

"I know what it is," Josh said. "It's just that I've read about the San Diego Zoo. It's, like, one of the biggest zoos in the whole world." His eyes glittered with the spark of an idea. "Hey, why don't you let me go there while you guys go to the park?"

"No," Robbie said flatly.

"But I don't want to listen to a bunch of girl gab," Josh said. "Yap-yap-yap, blab-blab-blab, giggle-giggle, oh, I like her hair, oh, isn't he cute—yeeech!"

Robbie, of course, knew what Josh was up to. Allen was probably in the trunk of the car, and the two of them weren't going to forget that strange signal. Then again, in an unfamiliar city without a car, what could they do except exchange unsupported conspiracies with each other? "Okay," Robbie said, realizing that Josh wouldn't be any fun in his present mood anyway. "We'll drop you off at the zoo if you promise not to get into trouble." She spoke with a significant

expression on her face, the one that clearly instructed Josh to keep a close watch on Allen.

"Gotcha," Josh acknowledged knowingly.

The parking lot of the San Diego Zoo was big enough to get lost in, but Vonda drove unerringly past row after row of neatly parked cars until she finally pulled up at the front entrance.

"Oh, wait a minute," said Robbie. "Tickets." She slumped. "We don't have enough money."

"No problem." Vonda reached into her purse and took out a twenty-dollar bill. "Here, Josh. Go wild."

Before Robbie could say a word, Josh snatched the bill up and hopped out of the car. "Thanks! Bye!" And he ran for the entrance.

Robbie glanced at her watch. "We'll pick you up at four o'clock!" she yelled after him.

By the time Vonda had driven to the main street again, Robbie was still looking back toward the zoo entrance. "You sure he'll be all right alone?" she asked with a twinge of worry.

"Robbie, the zoo is made for kids and it's full of people. He'll be okay as long as he doesn't try to hug a polar bear."

Robbie gulped. Josh wouldn't do that, but Allen might . . .

* * *

Josh watched Vonda's red convertible drive away. "Okay, it's all clear," he said to thin air. "Allen, where are you?"

"Over here." Allen emerged from behind a tree, rubbing his neck. "Riding in the trunk of the first car wasn't bad, but the convertible trunk was a little tight."

"Sports cars are supposed to be little," Josh said. "The less you can fit into them, the cooler they are. Now, c'mon, let's go catch the bus."

"Bus? I thought we were going in there," and Allen pointed at the zoo entrance.

"Are you kidding? Allen, we've got to get back to the bay and investigate that signal."

"What about Robbie?"

"What about her?"

"You promised her we'd stay here. She'll be coming to pick us up at four o'clock."

"So we'll be back here by four o'clock."

That seemed to satisfy Allen, who by now was used to Josh's more flexible way of looking at the world. "Okay."

"Great! Then let's catch the bus."

Allen took a step forward, then paused as a flock of children ran by, shrieking with excitement. Dozens of people were lined up at each of the ticket booths, waiting to get in. Everybody

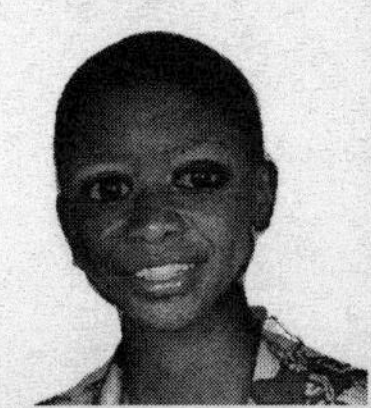

seemed happy to be there. "Can't we go in first, just to take a peek?" asked Allen. "I've never been to a zoo before."

"You don't have zoos on Xela?"

Allen shook his head.

"Oh, all right." Josh chose a line and beckoned Allen over. "We're going to deplete our resources," he said, waving Vonda's twenty-dollar bill, "but we should still have enough to buy bus tickets."

"You humans sure do need tickets for a lot of things," Allen noted.

"Yeah, and if that isn't bad enough, we usually have to stand in line to even get the tickets we want," said Josh. "Personally, I think it's a conspiracy."

"Who's behind it?" Allen asked, intrigued.

Josh beckoned for Allen to lean closer. "Adults," he whispered.

They bought tickets and walked through the wide, tunnellike entrance. The vast lush green expanse of the zoo grounds opened up before them like a landscaped jungle.

Josh plucked a free information pamphlet from a stand. "Hey, Allen, it says here that the San Diego Zoo was founded in 1916 by a Dr. Harry Wegeforth. He started it with fifty animals. Now it's got almost four thousand animals and eight hundred species—"

Allen gasped. "Pink birds!"

"Huh?" Josh looked up from the pamphlet. "Oh, those are flamingos. Pretty amazing color, huh? Grandma actually has plastic ones on her grass. Flamingos and lawn gnomes." He shuddered as his memory provided the unwanted mental picture.

Allen hurried over to the low-fenced area where several stately flamingos strutted before the appreciative crowd. "I've seen green birds and orange birds and birds of just about every color in the universe, but not pink." Allen couldn't take his eyes off them. "Their legs are so skinny! How do they stand up when the wind blows?"

"How should I know? Why don't you ask them?"

"Okay." Allen leaned as far over the fence as he could, staring hard at the nearest flamingo. Curious, it turned to face him, and then strutted over on its long sticklike legs until its big curved beak was almost touching the alien boy's nose. Xelan and flamingo gazed into each other's eyes as the crowd slowly realized that something odd was going on.

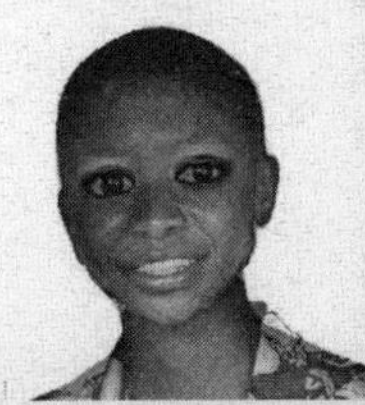

"Mommy!" said a little girl. "That boy is trying to kiss the birdie!"

Josh tapped Allen's shoulder. "Uh, Allen, I think you'd better cut the conversation short."

"Wait," Allen murmured without moving, "she's just getting to the good part."

"Allen!" Josh had to physically pull the alien boy away.

With a loud squawk, the flamingo ruffled its feathers, annoyed at having been interrupted. In reply, Allen imitated the bird's ruffling motions and uttered an impressive imitation of its squawk. The flamingo squawked back, and then all of the flamingos squawked once in unison.

The crowd laughed and applauded. Allen waved for their attention. "*Skviawkee* wants me to tell you all that she and her family are glad that so many humans come to the zoo," he said. "It's been a flamingo tradition to greet visitors here for years, and they really enjoy it."

The crowd laughed again, and Allen turned to Josh in confusion. "Why is that funny?"

"Allen, the story of Dr. Doolittle is a classic, but I don't think people are really ready to talk to the animals just yet. Let's go see the monkeys or something."

The two boys embarked on a whirlwind tour of

the zoo—not an easy task. The grounds comprised one hundred acres, and they covered nearly a third of it before Josh announced that it was time to go. "I'll be too exhausted to even ride the bus if we don't leave soon."

Of course, Allen had to say good-bye to every animal as he made his way back to the main entrance. "Good-bye, snakes," he said cheerfully, waving at the reptile cages. "Good-bye, peacocks. I really like the feathers. Good-bye koala bears." And to the colorful wild jungle fowl that roamed freely on the grounds, Allen said, "Good-bye, little chicken-things. Don't get trampled, okay?"

By the time they left the zoo, Josh was holding his fingers in his ears. "Allen, if you say good-bye to one more animal . . ." His voice trailed off and he froze, staring at something ahead.

Allen tried to see what had caught his friend's attention. "What is it?" he finally had to ask.

Josh pointed. "I don't believe it. That's Phil Berg!"

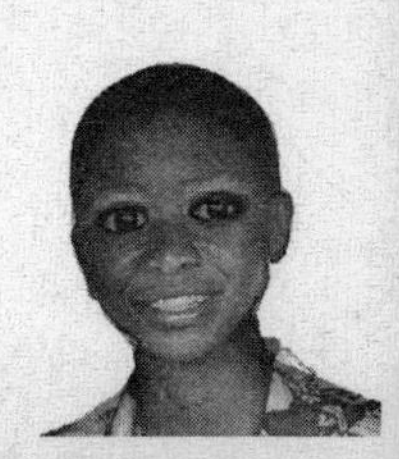

CHAPTER 7

2:05 P.M.
BALBOA PARK

"That narrow road over there is a service road that travels along one edge of the zoo and goes all the way to the rear of the Old Globe Theatre complex," said Vonda as she and Robbie walked from the parking lot to a large grassy area. "I've seen several plays by Shakespeare at the Globe, including *Hamlet* on the Cassius Carter Centre Stage. That's an outdoor stage, by the way. The production was really amazing."

"Oh," said Robbie. Already she was a little overwhelmed with information—Vonda was taking her job as tour guide seriously and spouting every fact she knew about everything they passed. As well, she'd fully informed Robbie of all the places they *weren't* going to visit in the park "because it's little boy stuff": the San Diego Aerospace Museum, Automotive Museum, Model Railroad Museum, Natural History Museum, and the Reuben H. Fleet Space Theater and Science Center. "But we can't miss the Botanical Building," she'd said, and so that was where they were heading first. Agreeable to just about any plan at this point, Robbie merely followed.

"Of course, there's another outdoor theater here in the park," Vonda said as they turned right at a huge splashing fountain. Robbie followed her down a long flight of concrete steps to a majestic walkway that spanned the heart of the park. "Over that way," and Vonda pointed left, "is the Starlight Bowl. It's right under the airport pathway, and whenever planes fly overhead they're so loud you can't hear the dialogue. So the actors freeze in place until the plane goes by, even if it's in the middle of a musical number."

Robbie envisioned an entire stage full of actors suddenly stopping at once, orchestra and all. "That must be pretty funny," she said, amused.

"It's not funny," Vonda stated. "It's theater."

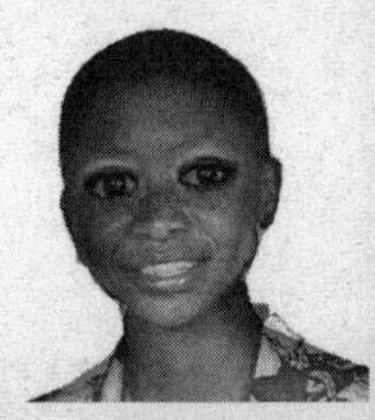

"Uh . . ." Robbie decided to say nothing.

A little more walking, and suddenly the Botanical Building appeared from around a corner on the right. Robbie didn't expect to see something the size of a castle, but that was almost what it looked like, except that the entire structure was open to the air; it was built of redwood lath and surrounded by palm and eucalyptus trees.

Like a carpet leading up to its front door, a long rectangular reflecting pool lay before the building, filled with luxuriant aquatic plants, plate-sized lily pads, and the biggest goldfish Robbie had ever seen. "Wow, Moby Dick the great white koi," she commented when several fish rose to the surface as if to check her out. After gulping greedily at the air for a moment, they sank back down into the murky depths so that Robbie could see only ghostly gold-and-white blurs.

"The Japanese used to raise koi in their backyards for food," Vonda said. "Did you know that?"

"Yup," Robbie replied. "My grandma's got a koi pond in her backyard, and she's always talking about eating one for lunch someday. But she never has. I think she's just kidding, because she likes them as pets too much."

Vonda blinked. "Oh."

She led Robbie into the Botanical Building and began to point out all the plants she recognized, even though they were labeled anyway. Robbie didn't have any particular interest in plants, but the garden was so lush and cool that she amiably followed Vonda along the quaint twisting path.

"I regularly come here to rest after my ballet class, which is held in the Casa del Prado, that building we passed earlier," Vonda explained at one point. "Sometimes I get a cup of tea from the Park Café and sit here and watch the tourists."

"You take ballet?" Robbie asked. "I'll bet that's fun. When I was little I considered taking ballet, but I got into surfing instead. Did your mom ever tell you that my mom was once a surfing champion?"

Vonda bristled. "No, I'm afraid she didn't," she said sharply. "I think the ocean is pretty to look at, but the classic arts are where it's at."

Robbie flinched but held her tongue. As nice as Vonda could be, she was starting to get irritating. She seemed to be trying to impress Robbie, but why she'd want to do that, Robbie had no idea.

"So what do you do when you're not taking ballet lessons and watching actors freeze onstage?"

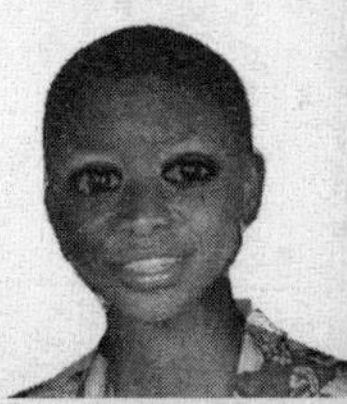

Robbie asked, aware too late of the sarcasm in her tone.

Vonda caught the sarcasm but chose to ignore it. "I like going to the mall."

Robbie couldn't resist pushing just a little more. "Really? I prefer the beach. It's more natural."

Vonda shrugged one shoulder. "To each her own, I guess," and she turned her back.

Now Robbie was sorry she'd baited Vonda. The last thing she wanted to do was start a fight, but she couldn't help wondering why the girl seemed so defensive—eager to please and yet easily angered. The whole situation confused Robbie, who just wanted to have a good time. "I know," Robbie finally suggested. "Why don't we get something to eat? I'm getting kind of hungry, aren't you?" Vonda appeared to think about it, so Robbie added, "It doesn't have to be anything big. We can just get a cheap snack."

Now Vonda grinned and, digging in her purse, pulled out her credit card. "How about we feast on plastic instead? And I know just the place!"

"That café you mentioned? It sounds kind of expensive."

"Nope, not the café." Making a beeline for the door, Vonda said, "The place I'm thinking of isn't in the park. We're going to Horton Plaza!"

"Wait! We're leaving the park?" Robbie asked. "What about Josh?"

"Oh, he's probably stuffing himself with peanuts and having a ball. HP's not far, and we've got plenty of time. C'mon, Robbie!"

Infused with new energy, Vonda hurried out of the Botanical Building and back to the parking lot. Robbie had no choice but to follow, though she did lodge a mild protest: "I've hardly seen the park yet. And you said there was a Museum of Photographic Arts." Robbie was taking a photography class at school, and she wanted to see that museum more than all the other places in the park.

"Maybe we can come back later," Vonda said, not slowing down. "But really, Horton Plaza is much more interesting anyway."

"Well . . . okay." Robbie got into the car and buckled her seat belt. "You're the tour guide."

"I certainly am." Vonda revved the engine and soon they were heading downtown.

Vonda clearly knew how to handle her car well, but Robbie noticed that she was going faster than before. Much faster. Robbie started to get nervous. "What's the speed limit?" she asked, trying to sound casual.

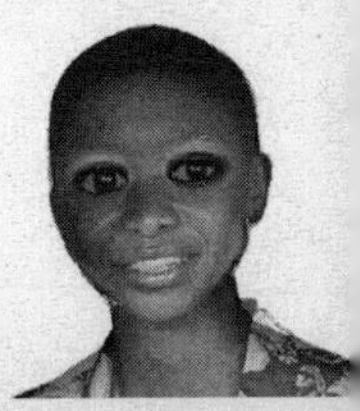

"Whatever I can get away with," answered Vonda. "Look, I confess that I drove like a granny when your brother was in the car because I don't trust little boys. They can't keep a secret to save their lives. I presume that you, on the other hand, can." She suddenly swerved, pulled over, and stopped.

Robbie was startled. "What are you doing? What's the matter?"

Her question answered itself as a police car cruised past. Vonda watched it, grinning. "I've got to keep my eyes peeled for cops," she said, as if it was a game. "I already got two speeding tickets this month."

"And your mom still lets you drive?" Robbie asked, shocked. "Boy, if it were my mom, I'd be so grounded."

Vonda's grin faded. "Yeah, well, how can my mom ground me if she doesn't know about it? I just paid them with this," and she held up her credit card again.

Robbie didn't know what to say. Didn't Vonda ever think that she might get into an accident? And how could she lie to her mother about the tickets? Didn't Pamela check her daughter's credit card statements every month, just to be sure? After all, she was paying the bills.

"Oh, don't look so upset," Vonda said as she pulled the car back out into traffic. "I'm almost a legal adult, you know." She hit the gas, again going too fast.

Robbie felt that she should say something, but she was too distracted by Vonda's driving. Vonda should have been using her brakes to go down the steep hills that led downtown, but instead Vonda hit the gas again, weaving dangerously close to a truck and then cutting sharply in front of a big SUV. The SUV driver honked, and Vonda honked back. With a gulp, Robbie tightened her seat belt and prayed that Horton Plaza wasn't too far away.

Fortunately, Vonda turned a few corners, and the strangest piece of architecture Robbie had ever seen come into view—Horton Plaza shopping mall. A mass of earth-toned masonry decorated with wildly colorful borders, banners, and signs, the mall spanned six city blocks and looked like a medieval fortress designed by a Las Vegas showman. Vonda parked and led Robbie into the bowels of the open-air mall, where shoppers strolled along a maze of walkways, staircases, and ramps that led to a wide variety of stores. "It's like Wonderland in here," Robbie said, dazzled by the colorful clutter around her.

"This is the coolest shopping mall in the city,"

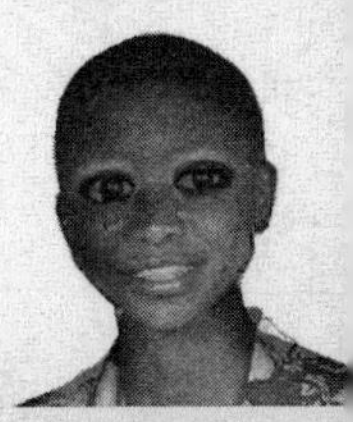

said Vonda. "If you like to spend money, this is the place to do it."

Robbie didn't particularly want to spend money, but Vonda said, "Don't be such a stick-in-the-mud. Let's have some fun! The restaurants are up here." She led the way to the top level of the mall where Robbie was greeted by a beautiful view of the bay on one side and an impressive panorama of downtown San Diego on the other. "Let's do Chinese," suggested Vonda.

"In a sit-down place?" Robbie asked. "That can get awfully expensive."

"Don't worry. It's on Mom!"

Reluctant but cornered, Robbie followed Vonda into a fancy Chinese restaurant, remembering back when she'd thought that spending an afternoon with a teen who drove her own car would be great. Instead, she was starting to feel more and more uneasy.

Why was Vonda acting like this? One minute she seemed really nice, and the next minute she personified the word "idiot." And she'd certainly made one point clear: she liked to spend her mother's money.

What was her problem?

CHAPTER 8

2:20 P.M.
BALBOA PARK

Allen did a double take. "Phil Berg, the alien hunter? He's here? Josh, we've got to go!"

"No, it's not like that," said Josh, and he took off down the path leading from the zoo entrance to the Balboa Park grounds. Hesitantly Allen followed, though he wondered why Josh would actually want to see Phil Berg. And then he realized that it wasn't really Phil Berg the boy had seen.

At the edge of the walkway, a tall, gangly man was standing next to a newspaper that had been pasted to a board, like a big poster. "The

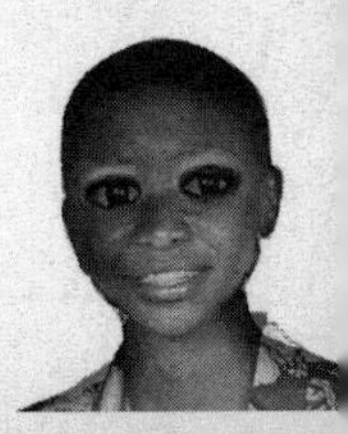

Free-kly," Allen read, "San Diego's Leading Conspiracy Rag?"

"You got it," said the gangly man. "It's free and it's a weekly, hence the name. Clever, eh? Oh, I see you're already a fan of our new columnist." These last words were directed at Josh, who happened to be wearing his *Watch the Skies* T-shirt. "You a Berg fan?"

"Sort of," Josh said, studying the picture of Phil Berg on the front page of the *Free-kly.* The bizarre host of Delport's cable program *Watch the Skies* looked just as goofy in the photo as he did on the air. What he considered a friendly smile looked more like a grimace, and an aura of compulsive fanaticism radiated from his newsprint eyes. "I didn't know Berg wrote for a newspaper," Josh said.

"He's just starting this week," the man answered, obviously pleased by the fact. "He'll be doing a column on alien conspiracies in every other issue. No Berg fan should be without the debut issue. Here, have one." He handed a copy over.

"Free?" Josh asked, taking it. "Thanks."

"You want one?" the man asked Allen.

Allen shook his head. "No, thanks. I know too much about Berg already."

The man's expression perked up and he opened his mouth to speak. Josh said quickly, "Well, thanks. Bye! C'mon, Allen."

As they hurried away, Allen read aloud the headline over Berg's picture: "'I Was Abducted by Aliens! You Can Be, Too!' Strange. You'd think his experience with the Trykloids would have straightened him out."

"Hardly," Josh said. "I don't think he was flying on all thrusters in the first place. His brain's gotta be spaghetti by now."

They reached a bus kiosk and, after consulting the schedule, learned that a bus heading for the San Diego Bay area would be coming by in only a few minutes. "Perfect timing," Josh crowed when it arrived. They boarded and took seats in the back.

"Josh," Allen asked, "exactly what are we going to do when we get there?"

"Snoop," answered Josh. "Actually, it'll depend on whether you can pick up that signal again or not." As the bus began to move down Park Avenue, he started reading Berg's column. But he was hardly a paragraph into it when the headline next to it caught his eye: "Signal Disruptions at San Diego Bay—Power Poles or Conspiracy?" Amazed, Josh thrust the

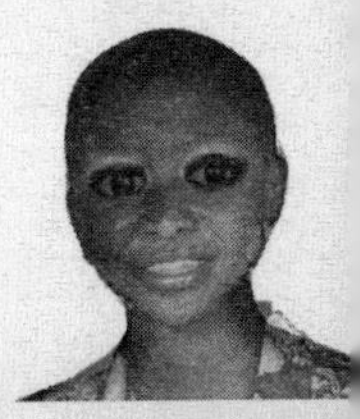

newspaper into Allen's face. "Allen, check it out!"

Allen did. "Hey, do you think—?"

"I don't know." Josh began to read aloud: "'Have you ever wondered why your radio goes static when you pass the bay?'"

"Like the radio in Pamela's car," said Allen.

Nodding, Josh continued. "'Ever wonder why residents of Point Loma can't get clear TV reception? The *Free-kly* has discovered the answer, and it all has to do with the secret history of San Diego Bay.'" Josh's eyes popped wide. "Allen, I think we're on to something."

"Keep reading," Allen urged.

> "*Free-kly* journalists have uncovered evidence that back during World War II, a load of experimental radar-guided torpedoes, destined for transfer aboard a naval ship accidentally sank while en route to the Thirty-second Street Naval Station in San Diego Bay. The entire shipment was lost. To cover their blunder, the navy denied charges that such experimental weaponry ever existed. The torpedoes have been corroding somewhere under the water for fifty years now, and the process has caused them to build up

an electrical charge too faint yet for human sensing equipment to detect. But *Free-kly* journalists believe that the charge exists. The failure of radio and TV reception in the area proves it. It is speculated that such an electrical charge could set the torpedoes off if it grew strong enough."

Josh paused. "I don't like the sound of that." Allen just said, "Keep going."

"Such a dangerous scenario would normally be unlikely. However, with all of the high-powered equipment in use by the navy in the area, who's to say what might prove to be the Trigger of Destruction? As well, rumors abound of the secret naval installations that honeycomb the Point Loma coast. Could equipment in use there—equipment the American public knows nothing about—trigger doomsday? If the U.S. Navy is being truthful and no such experimental weaponry existed fifty years ago, then we at the *Free-kly* will admit our mistake. But if we're right, how long will it be before San Diego Bay explodes?"

* * *

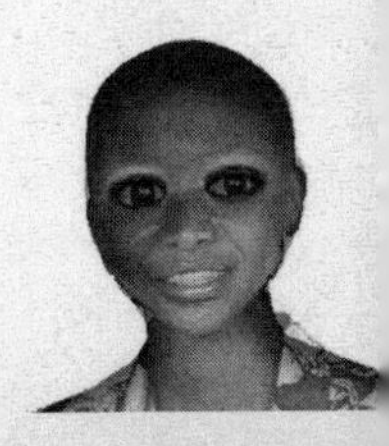

Josh set the paper down. "Whoa."

A moment of silence passed as the two boys digested the possibilities. The bus continued down Park Avenue, then turned onto Broadway. At the next stop, three girls with matching pink suits and purple hair got on, but neither boy noticed, even when one of the girls accidentally knocked Josh in the head with her purse when she walked past. Too lost in thought, the boys just kept turning over the *Free-kly* information in their minds until Allen said, "Do you think this has anything to do with the signal I sensed?"

"Have you ever heard the word 'duh?'"

Allen fidgeted in his seat. "Yeah, but . . . what if Robbie's right? What if we're just feeding each other's imagination? This article could be a complete coincidence."

Josh stared into Allen's eyes. "Do you really believe that?"

Allen considered it carefully. "Not really," he decided.

"Then let's get off at the next stop. We're almost there."

The next bus stop happened to be right across the street from the AmeriTrak station. "This looks familiar," said Allen, following Josh across the street. They ran all the way to the Cruise Ship Terminal where they'd boarded the harbor tour boat earlier that morning.

"Okay, we've got to find a place for you to turn into your light body so you can search for the signal," said Josh.

Allen thought of Superman. "How about a phone booth?"

"Too small. I know—a restaurant." He scanned the boardwalk. "There's one. C'mon!"

Antonio's Fish Grotto was right on the shore. It looked pretty ritzy, but the boys casually strolled in without being stopped—Josh knew how to put that "I'm looking for my parents" expression on his face. Once they found the rest room, he gestured Allen inside. "You know what to do. I'll stand guard."

Moments later, Josh pretended not to notice the brilliant white light that leaked out from under the men's room door. When an elderly gentleman approached, he said, "Uh, sir, there's an electrical problem in there. I'm waiting for the attendant."

"I'm not here for a light show," the man said with a wink.

Josh tried to sound sincere. "The plumbing's out, too."

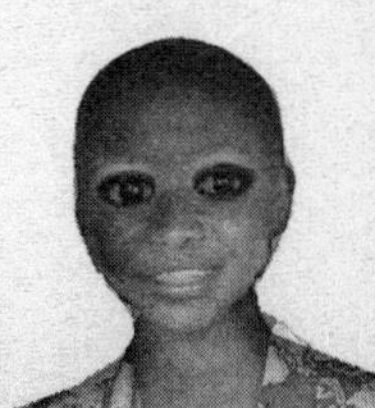

With an aggravated grunt, the man nodded and left. Josh sighed in relief.

Just then Allen came out.

"So?" Josh prodded him.

Allen's wide eyes gave the answer before his words did. "Oh, I felt it, all right. Real strong. It is *not* my imagination. But neither is it the *jbypidoch* signal."

"How can you be so sure?"

"Because I sensed *two* signals this time."

That took Josh by surprise. *"What?"*

"I don't understand it. They're the same signal, but they're coming from two different places." Allen pointed west. "A strong one from that direction"—he pointed again, this time south—"and a weaker signal from that direction."

The boys left the restaurant and hurried down to the boardwalk. Josh used his bus map to find the source area that Allen had indicated. "West of here is Point Loma," he concluded, "that peninsula over there, remember? That's where NOSC is."

Using his hand to shade his eyes from the glare of the sun, Allen gazed across the bay to Point Loma. "The Naval Operations Surveillance Command. Yes, that would make sense. The stronger of the two signals could be emanating from a sensor device employed by NOSC."

"Or by one of those secret naval installations the tour guide told us about," Josh added.

"If the device in question only put out a signal intermittently, that would explain why I don't always sense it." Allen turned south. "What's that way?"

Josh shrugged. "Mexico?"

Allen shook his head, clearly confused. "I don't understand why I would be sensing the same signal from two different . . ." His voice trailed off and his eyes lit up. "Unless the second signal is actually an *echo!*"

For once, Josh had to admit that he didn't get it.

"What if there's something out there that's catching the signal, absorbing most of the energy, but bouncing back just enough for me to detect?" Allen glanced at the copy of the *Free-kly* in Josh's hands. "I've got an idea how to find out."

Allen hurried over to the boardwalk railing and peered down. The gentle waves of the bay splashed up against the concrete wall about twenty feet below. "Energy travels through water differently than it travels through air," he said. "I might be able to sense the echo better if I touch the water."

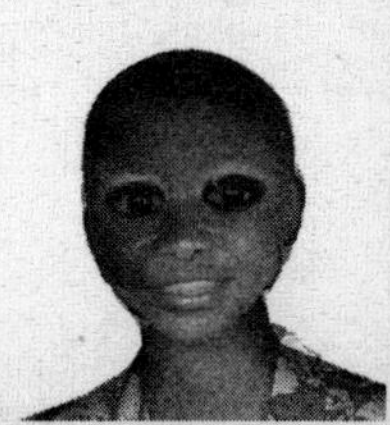

"But you can't," said Josh. "Unless your arm's a mile long."

Calculating quickly, Allen said, "No, I think eighteen point three feet will do." With that, he leaned over the rail and extended his right arm. It began to stretch out longer and longer until his hand touched the water far below.

Josh was pretty used to Allen's powers by now, but every once in a while the alien caught him off guard. This was one of those times. "Whoa!" he spluttered. "Your arm's growing!"

"No, it's just stretching," Allen corrected. He closed his eyes to concentrate, and the next thing Josh knew, Allen's stretched-out arm had shifted into its pure light form. Allen froze in that position, his light hand searching the water for the signal as Josh wildly looked around the boardwalk, hoping nobody was around to witness this. Actually, there were lots of people nearby. Fortunately, they were all in cars, so no one noticed Allen's long, rubbery arm or the glowing hand at the end of it.

"I sense it," Allen reported. "The signal from Point Loma is bouncing off several metal objects at the bottom of the bay several miles south of here." He paused, calculating. "The objects are buried pretty deep, but judging by the configuration of the bounce-back signal, they could be the size of torpedoes. The electrical charge around them is slowly growing stronger."

"The *Free-kly* article said that the torpedoes could detonate if a big enough electrical charge built up around them," Josh said uneasily.

As Allen restored his stretched-out arm to normal, an even more horrible thought occurred to him. "Josh, do you remember what the harbor guide said during our tour? Didn't she say that the strip of beach south of here—"

"The Silver Strand," Josh offered.

"Yes, the Silver Strand. Didn't she say it was *mined?*"

Josh's face went pale. Slowly he nodded. "If those torpedoes go off . . ."

"And they're anywhere near those mines . . ."

Josh checked his watch, then consulted his bus schedule. "We've got to get back to the zoo. Robbie and Vonda will be there to pick us up soon. We've got to warn them!"

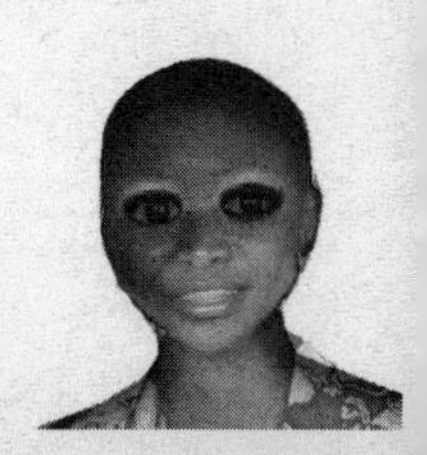

CHAPTER 9

3:22 P.M.
HORTON PLAZA SHOPPING CENTER
DOWNTOWN SAN DIEGO

"So I told her I wanted my own credit card," Vonda said, poking at her plate of cashew chicken with her chopsticks. "I have a lot to do, and I want access to money without having to chase her around asking for it all the time. It's great—I buy, she pays."

Robbie toyed with her chow mein. She'd tried to use chopsticks but couldn't get the hang of it, so she was using a fork. Still, she wasn't eating much despite being so hungry. A sad picture of Vonda's life was forming in her head, and she didn't like what she saw.

"Of course, I couldn't believe it when she actually got me one," Vonda continued. "I mean, I just asked one day and she said okay. Would your mom do that?"

"No way," said Robbie.

"So anyway, what happens when I get it? I end up doing all the shopping. But I don't mind because I buy what I want and to heck with what she wants." Vonda seemed pleased with herself. "And with Dad's old car, I can go wherever I want whenever I want. Frankly, I consider myself an adult already. The second I'm eighteen, I'm outta that stupid house."

"Why?" Robbie asked, truly curious. The Burkes' house was great, and Vonda seemed to already have all the freedom a teenager could want.

Vonda, however, didn't think so. "What do you mean, *why?* Because I *can.* Hey, want to go shopping after we're done here?"

Robbie hesitated. "I'd love to, but I'm kind of on a budget."

"Excuse me, but what have we been talking about? I know—let me buy you a present. Some cool jeans, or some shoes. I know a great store."

"No," Robbie said, "that's okay."

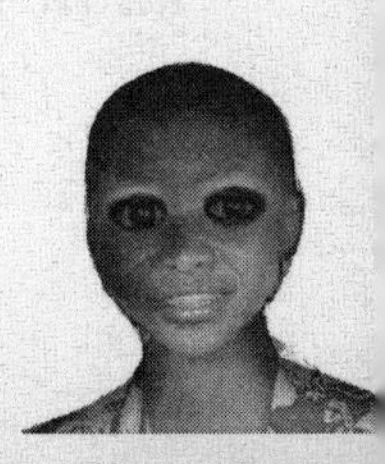

A dark shadow crossed Vonda's eyes. "What . . . don't you like me?"

Robbie was shocked. "What? Liking you has nothing to do with it."

"I'm offering you free stuff. What more do you want?"

Robbie had no idea what to say. No matter how hard she tried to relate to Vonda, she ended up making her angry. "Vonda, we need to talk about something."

"No, we don't," said Vonda. "I'm not blind, you know. I can see what you're thinking. Poor Vonda, her mom has abandoned her." Vonda shifted her voice to sound more like Pamela. "'I'm sorry, honey, but I have a meeting.' 'I can't go with you, sweetheart. I have to work.' 'I won't be home till late tonight, pumpkin, so fix yourself some dinner.'" Vonda gulped a mouthful of soda. "That's all I hear. I'm living alone already, so what's the difference?"

"Doesn't your dad ever come around?"

"Not if he doesn't have to." Vonda studied Robbie's face. "Hey, don't wig out over it. You wouldn't understand. You're younger than I am, and your parents still talk to each other."

That stung Robbie. "That doesn't mean I don't know how you feel."

With a patronizing smile, Vonda said, "Thanks for trying, but no, you *don't* know how I feel. You're still a kid."

That was the last straw. With slow, deliberate movements, Robbie set down her fork, folded her napkin, and stood up. "I think we ought to go now."

"Oh, now she's mad."

Robbie sat back down. "Vonda, I'm not mad so much as concerned. Don't you love your mom?"

Vonda actually had to think about it. "Yeah," she decided.

"Well, it looks to me like you're doing everything you can to ruin your relationship with her."

"I'm living my life," Vonda snapped, "and I don't need you or anybody else to tell me how to do it!" She was trembling with anger, and Robbie dared not speak until the girl calmed down.

"I'm sorry," Robbie finally said in a quiet voice.

Pulling out her wallet and slapping down her credit card, Vonda said, "Don't be."

After paying and leaving a generous cash tip, Vonda headed for the door. "It's time to pick up your brother."

Robbie just nodded and followed her out.

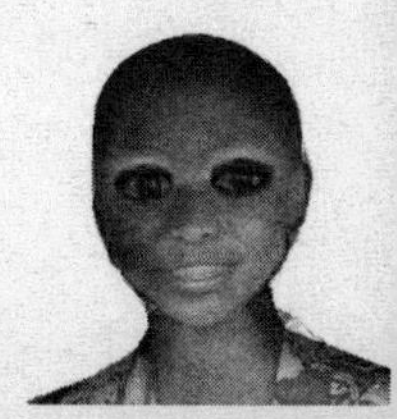

The ride back to the zoo was harrowing. Vonda drove more recklessly than before, weaving and honking and speeding until Robbie almost shouted at her. But Vonda was clearly on the edge. Without meaning to, Robbie had tapped into all her buried frustrations, and like a bomb, Vonda was on the verge of exploding. Robbie had no intention of setting her off.

When they pulled up to the zoo entrance, Josh was there waiting. He ran to the car. "Robbie!" he yelled. "Robbie, I gotta talk to *you!*"

Robbie did a double take, pretending to be surprised. "Uh, gee, Josh, who's that *with you?*"

"Huh?" Too late Josh realized what she meant. The person in question hadn't become invisible like he was supposed to. Instead he was waving at Vonda. "Hello!" Allen said in his cheerfully musical voice.

Robbie groaned. Josh fidgeted. Vonda just cocked her head. "Who're you?"

"I'm Allen—"

"A friend of ours," Josh cut in. "He's from Delport. I, uh, ran into him in the zoo. Pretty coincidental, huh?"

"Human lives are full of coincidences," Allen added helpfully.

"They sure are," Robbie said in a low voice, glaring daggers at Josh.

Josh leaned close to her. "Don't get mad until you hear what we've discovered," he whispered. "This whole city could blow sky high any minute!"

Robbie snorted. "Josh, did you hit your head on a hippo?"

"No, but a girl on the bus hit his head with her purse," Allen whispered.

"Girl *on the bus?*" Robbie frowned. "Josh, don't tell me you—"

"Okay, I won't. Besides, there's no time to argue about it. We've got to do something!"

"We certainly have," Robbie agreed. "We've got to get back to Vonda's house before Mom and Pamela come home from the conference."

"But, Robbie—"

"Excuse me, people," Vonda said loudly and pointedly. "Can I be a part of this conversation?"

Allen smiled at her. "No."

Thinking fast, Robbie said, "What Allen means is that I forgot about a really important homework assignment and he's just telling me about it. Believe me, you don't want to know."

Vonda rattled her car keys. "Well, if we don't

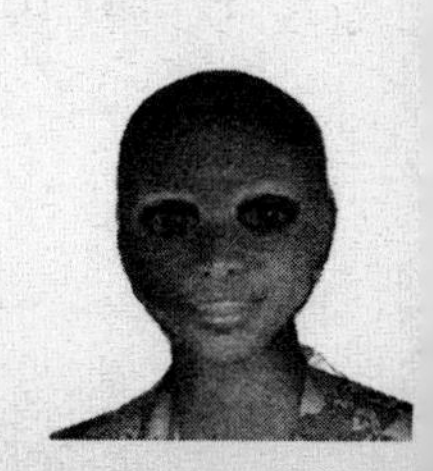

get moving soon, we'll be caught in rush-hour traffic."

Robbie gave Allen a significant look. "Well, then, Allen, I guess we'll see you back at Delport after the weekend. Thanks for reminding me about that assignment."

"But, Robbie," Allen began, then he stopped. "Oh. Right. See you Monday." To Vonda he said, "It was nice meeting you."

"Sure thing," said Vonda.

The second she turned her attention to the car, Allen shifted into his light form and phased into the trunk.

Robbie settled down in her seat as Josh leaped into the back. "Okay, let's go."

Vonda drove more slowly on the way back to Coronado Island, obviously not sure yet whether Josh could be trusted to keep her real driving habits a secret. Robbie was grateful that she didn't have to fear for her life this time, so she did the next best thing: she feared for Josh's life, because she intended to wring his neck when they got back to the Burkes' house.

It wasn't that he'd disobeyed her. Robbie wasn't a shining star in the obedience department, either. It was the fact that he'd gone off with Allen in an unfamiliar city without telling anybody. If anything had happened to either of them, she would have taken the heat for it.

She figured out easily enough that the two boys had ridden the bus back to the bay, but what had Josh meant when he'd said the city could blow sky high? Did Allen find actual evidence of one of those Trykloid japiddyboops, or whatever they were called? She couldn't help but be curious along with being angry.

Thank goodness Vonda seemed to take the conversation in stride. She was an odd girl, no doubt about it. She was so intent on ruining her own life that she didn't much care what anybody else did. Still, Robbie knew that Vonda was annoyed about the conversation they had had at lunch. Robbie hadn't meant to pry or interfere; she'd wanted to help. Vonda just didn't see it that way.

When they got back to the Burkes' house, Vonda went to her room to freshen up. Josh pulled Robbie to the kitchen. "Allen," the boy whispered loudly, "the coast is clear."

Allen's light head popped up from the kitchen sink. His light-particle body drifted up out of the drain, and he coalesced into his familiar human form. "It's disgusting down there," he reported with a grimace.

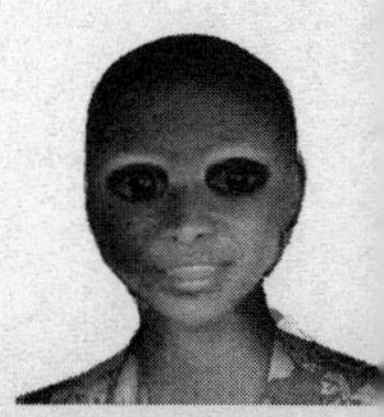

"Garbage disposal units usually are," said Robbie.

Allen's eyes lit up with understanding. "Ah. No wonder." He ran his hands down the front of his T-shirt. "I'm glad gelatinous scum doesn't stick to my Xelan form."

"Cut the home tour," Josh reprimanded him. "What are we going to do about those torpedoes?"

Robbie rolled her eyes. "Josh, I am telling you, there are no torpedoes in San Diego Bay. If there were—"

"Okay, you want proof? Then take a look at this." Josh produced his copy of the *Free-kly* from his jacket pocket. "Read the third article down."

Robbie took the paper, glanced over it, and laughed. "You believe something with Phil Berg's picture on it?"

"Berg has nothing to do with it!" Josh hissed in irritation.

Allen held up his hands. "Time out." He turned to Robbie. "You're right to doubt the *Free-kly,* but the fact is, I really did sense metallic devices buried under the water, and there really is an electrical charge building up around them. It's not strong enough yet for human technology to detect, but by the time it is, it may be too late."

"If those torpedoes blow, they could take the mines along the Silver Strand with them," Josh explained.

"The initial explosion wouldn't be the only catastrophe," continued Allen. "The resulting tidal forces could inundate the entire downtown area."

"And then there's the government's response to worry about," Josh said. "Can you imagine? Washington would go nuts thinking it was an attack or something."

"All in all, not a good scenario," Allen concluded.

"Okay, okay." Robbie did her best to comprehend the potential calamity. "Let's say you guys are right. What can we do to prevent a disaster?"

"Evacuate the city," said Josh without hesitation. "Call in the National Guard."

"We could also call in Superman," Robbie snapped, "but this happens to be the real world. Oops, I forgot—you only have a visitor's pass."

"Har-har," Josh snapped back. "This is serious."

"What's serious?" came Vonda's voice. Robbie and Josh whirled around to find Vonda in the

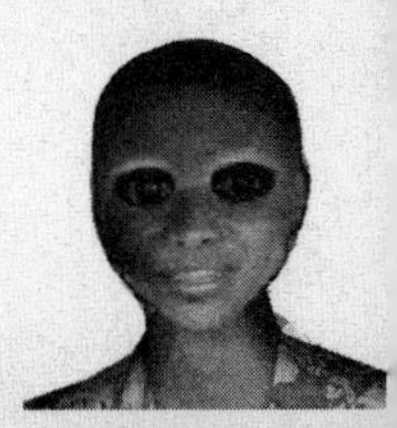

kitchen doorway. "You guys sure like to whisper a lot," she said. "What is with you, anyway?"

Casting a quick glance behind her to make sure that Allen had indeed disappeared this time, Robbie said brightly, "We were just discussing how important it is that . . . that I start my assignment right away." Pleased at the white lie, Robbie added, "You know, the one Allen told me about at the zoo. I'm always putting things off, but Josh here tries to keep me on the right track." She playfully punched her brother in the shoulder. "Don't you, Josh?"

Josh opened his mouth to say something—probably something sarcastic—but Robbie never heard what it was. At that moment, Pamela's car pulled into the driveway. Robbie spotted it through the kitchen window and sprinted for the door. "They're home! C'mon!"

"We're not through with this!" Josh yelled, dashing after her.

Vonda watched them, puzzled. "I'm definitely glad I'm an only child."

CHAPTER 10

8:05 P.M.
THE BURKES' HOUSE
CORONADO ISLAND

"A devoted fan from Hiskatonee, Wisconsin, writes, 'Dear Phil Berg, Abduction Expert and Alien Hunter. What is it with aliens, anyway? Why can't they just leave Earth alone?' Signed, Olaf Skorskyv . . . skyv . . . vtiltsk . . . oh, whatever the heck it is."

Phil Berg leaned in close to the TV camera so that his face filled the screen. Chewing a mouthful of gum so noisily that the microphone clipped to his shirt pocket popped and crackled like static, he drawled, "All righty, Olaf, listen up.

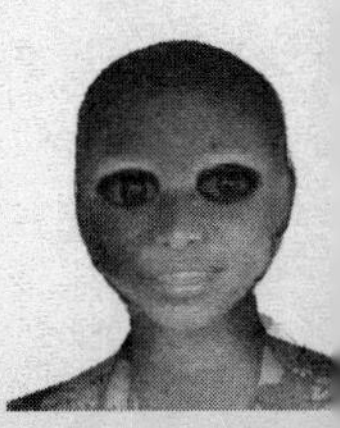

The thing you have to understand about aliens is that they're basically paranoid. Why do they want to conquer our planet? Because they're *afraid* of us! Oh sure, we might not have superior technology yet, but they know we'll be far superior to them in the future."

Vonda nudged Josh's shoulder. "You watch this freak on a regular basis?"

"Yeah," Josh answered, not moving from his spot on the floor, his eyes glued to the TV screen less than ten inches away. "Berg's got more insight than most people realize."

Vonda leaned back in the sofa, muttering, "How does Robbie put up with you?"

In the kitchen, Robbie was helping her mother wash the dinner dishes. Pamela had discreetly left to sort some laundry, Josh was absorbed in Berg's show, and Vonda was trapped in the living room with him, so Robbie had some time alone with her mother.

"I haven't seen you in so long, Mom," she said, drying a plate. "If it hadn't been for this conference, I might never have seen you again."

"Oh, I'm not so sure about that," Gail said, "but work has kept me pretty busy lately. It's summertime. People go a little crazy when they're on vacation. There have been more accidents than usual."

"Like people driving too fast and stuff?"

Gail thought about it. "Yes, that's one way to end up in the trauma ward of a hospital. So how was the tour today? Is Vonda a good guide?"

"She certainly knows the city," said Robbie, steering clear of any mention of the fact that Josh had taken his own private tour. "We covered a lot of ground."

"Good. Did you and she get along okay?"

"I guess." Robbie slowly placed another dried dish on the stack. "Mom, can I ask you something?"

"Sure."

"Why do you think you and I get along so well?"

The question caught Gail off guard. "Because I'm your mom and you're my kid?" she ventured.

"No, I mean, with you and Dad separated and everything, how come you and I still get along?"

"Why shouldn't we?" Then Gail put two and two together. "Oh, this is about Vonda and Pam, isn't it?"

Robbie nodded.

Lowering her voice, Gail said, "Robbie, I have

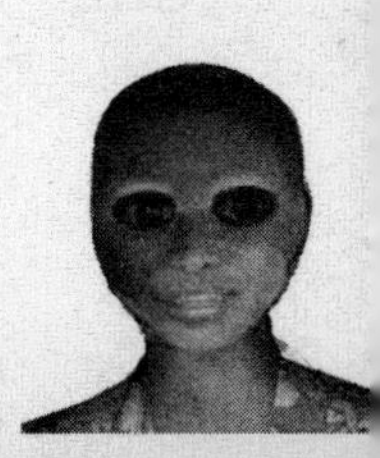

a confession to make. The main reason I came to San Diego was to see Pam. The conference just gave me a good excuse. Pam's divorce hit her hard, and it hit Vonda even harder. I wanted a chance to show them both that it can all work out."

"Do you really think it can?" asked Robbie. "I mean, Vonda hates her mother, and her mom doesn't seem to care."

"No, Robbie, that's not true. Pam and Vonda are a lot like you and me. It's just that"—Gail chose her words carefully—"it's just that Vonda responded to her parents' separation with anger."

Robbie said a little guiltily, "So did I."

"Not like Vonda," Gail assured her. "She's letting her anger make her reckless and mean. That's not how she really is. Pam can't see it because she's too busy avoiding her own pain by burying herself in her job. The two of them have a lot to work out, but I'm sure they'll make it. It'll just take time. Until then they need friends to talk to. They need to see that other mothers and daughters have gone down the same path and come out okay." Tossing the dish towel onto the counter, Gail drew Robbie into a hug. "I'm sorry this is making our visit awkward. I didn't think the Burkes' problems would have an impact on you and Josh. Maybe I shouldn't have invited you down."

"No, it's okay," Robbie said, hugging her mom. "Any chance to see you is great. Besides, I'm glad to hear that Vonda isn't really a jerk after all."

Gail couldn't help but chuckle. "Please don't tell her that."

"I promise—I won't."

Later that night after everyone had gone to bed, Robbie tiptoed downstairs to the kitchen. She found the stove light still on, illuminating the kitchen table with a soft golden glow while the far corners of the room faded away in shadow.

Vonda was sitting at the table nursing a cup of cocoa. "I thought you went to sleep," she commented when Robbie entered.

"I thought you were still in the bathroom," Robbie countered playfully.

"Just because you wash your face as fast as Josh does," Vonda snapped. "It's a wonder your skin doesn't look like the surface of the moon."

The last thing Robbie wanted was an argument. She'd meant her comment as a joke. "Hey, I'm sorry. I just came down for some water." She walked over to the cupboard, noting from the corner of her eye how Vonda just sat like a stat-

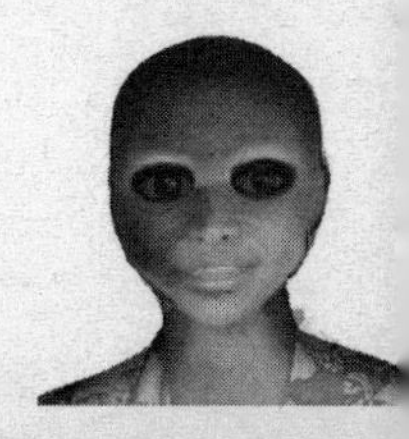

ue in the dim light. "I always wake up in the middle of the night thirsty," Robbie continued, hoping to smooth over her blunder with casual chat. "Do you do that?"

Vonda took a long sip of her cocoa. "No."

Robbie got a glass and filled it up from the sink. "You know, Vonda, contrary to what you think, you mom really does love you."

"Look, will you just drop it?"

Robbie set her glass down. It was a challenge to calm the rapid beating of her heart and to tamp down the anger that tightened her throat, but she managed it. Whirling on Vonda, she said quietly but distinctly, "No, I will *not* drop it."

The sharp tone of her voice startled Vonda.

"It doesn't matter that I'm a year younger than you," Robbie went on. "It doesn't matter that our circumstances are different. I know how you feel, and I think that what you're doing is wrong."

Vonda's eyes narrowed, but before she could figure out what to say, Robbie continued: "If you're angry at your mom, then talk to her. Don't take your anger out on yourself by acting like a brat and driving like a jerk, and don't take it out on me by scaring me to death and lecturing me all the time. And what's with spending your mom's money? It's like you're trying to take revenge or something. I mean, don't you think I'm angry, too? I hate my family situation as much as you hate yours, but getting angry about it doesn't help. In fact, it makes things worse. When my mom first left, I was so mad I wrecked my grades and messed up my whole life. But I met a friend . . ." She paused, surprised at her own words. "I met a friend whose situation was far worse than mine or yours, yet he's always cheerful and tries to do his best, and he . . . well, he saved me, I guess. He showed me the difference between being a victim of fate and making your own fate. I'd rather make my own fate." Robbie picked up her glass of water. "You can make yours too," she remarked, fleeing from the kitchen.

She wasn't sure how long she sat at the window in Vonda's room. She just sat in the silence of midnight, gazing up at the stars, feeling sorry for Vonda, and feeling terribly grateful that an alien called Allen Strange had come into her life.

From her angle at the window, she could see Pam's car parked below in the driveway. From inside the closed trunk, she could also see the hint of a sparkling bluish light that quietly pulsed, as though breathing. "Not exactly a

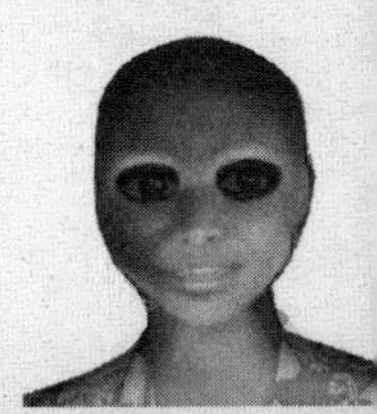

Lemorian Dream Pod," she murmured, "but I guess it'll do. Good night, Allen. Sleep tight."

She finally crawled into her sleeping bag on the floor and tried to go to sleep.

Just as a pleasant muzziness settled over her troubled thoughts, the door of the bedroom opened very quietly. Stealthy footsteps made their way to the bed, and the springs squeaked ever so softly. The sounds brought Robbie's mind back to wakefulness, but she didn't dare move. She didn't even open her eyes. Perhaps it was best if she and Vonda didn't talk anymore. Robbie had the feeling she'd already said enough. Maybe too much.

Then Vonda spoke. Her voice sounded strangely distant, as if she were talking, not to Robbie, but to someone else. "She used to take me out on the boat all the time. It was so much fun . . ." Her voice trailed off.

Robbie could imagine Vonda and Pamela out on their boat together, the laughing sun above them, the mischievous waves rolling beneath their feet. The mental image melted into a familiar shoreline. "We used to walk along the beach," Robbie found herself saying dreamily.

"She'd take me shopping."

"We'd go surfing."

"Whenever I was sick, she'd arrange all my stuffed animals around me in bed."

"She gave me a bead set and taught me how to make jewelry."

Silence. Robbie waited, but Vonda said nothing more. And then, soft as a whisper, came a sound. A sob. Vonda sniffed, then Robbie heard her inhale quickly and hold her breath, as though trying to stifle more sobs. It didn't work.

Robbie tried to shut out the sound of Vonda's crying. She searched her mind for something to say, but words seemed useless at this point. She just lay there in her sleeping bag and, for the first time in her life, wished she was sharing a room with Josh.

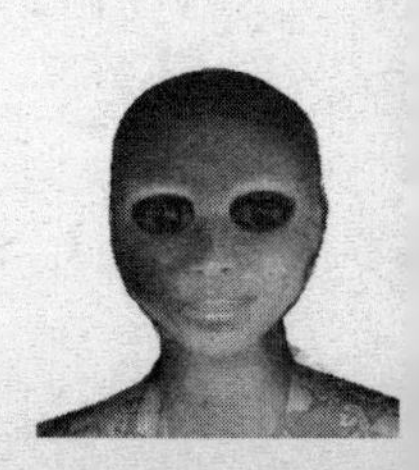

CHAPTER 11

8:13 A.M.
SUNDAY, JULY 4
THE BURKES' HOUSE

When Robbie woke up the next morning, her mother was already gone. The night before, Gail had said that she and Pamela would be getting up extra early to attend breakfast with their colleagues before the second day of the conference began. They planned to be back by six o'clock that afternoon for the Fourth of July evening festivities.

Josh was still asleep on the couch in the den, so Robbie headed for the kitchen. The last thing she expected to see was exactly what she did see: Vonda at the stove, cooking breakfast. Neither girl knew what to say at first. Vonda finally broke the silence. "Good morning."

"Good morning," Robbie replied. She decided she had to test the waters one way or another, so she gestured at the skillet of sizzling pancakes and said, "I figured you'd want to go out and eat at a restaurant."

Vonda bowed her head. At first Robbie thought she was trying to hide anger, but when the girl raised her head again, she said lightly, "Yeah, that's usually my first choice, but today I decided to save Mom's money."

A wave of relief swept over Robbie. She grinned. "Can I help?"

Vonda pointed to the refrigerator. "If you want to. Get the eggs. How does your mutant brother like them cooked?"

"Who cares?" Robbie said wickedly. "He'll eat what we put in front of him."

Vonda looked hard at Robbie, as if making a quick evaluation of where she stood. Apparently the results were good because she started to laugh. Robbie joined in.

The doorbell rang, and Josh came flying around the corner in his bathrobe. "I'll get it!" He bounded to the door and heaved it open to reveal Allen as the girls joined the boys.

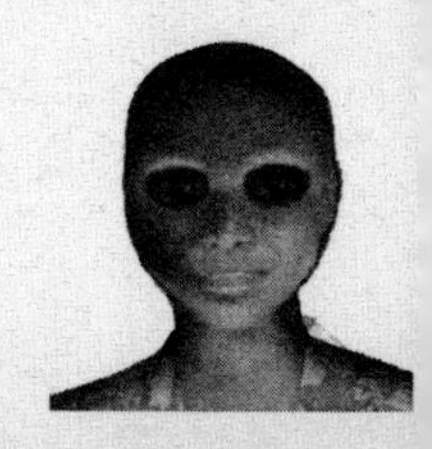

"Good morning," Allen greeted everyone.

Vonda's jaw dropped. "Isn't that your friend from the zoo? What's he doing at my house?"

"I invited him to breakfast," Josh said. "That's okay, isn't it?" He sniffed the air, then asked Allen, "You like pancakes, right?"

"Sure!" Allen said hungrily.

Vonda pursed her lips and seemed about to argue, but one glance at Robbie, who just shrugged helplessly, made her relax. She headed back to the kitchen, muttering, "Little boys . . ."

"Allen, why are you here, really?" Robbie quietly asked the alien once Vonda was out of earshot.

"I'm here for breakfast, really," Allen replied. "I like pancakes."

"No, I mean . . . oh, never mind." Robbie turned to Josh. "I guess it's okay, but let me know next time. Allen shouldn't be around Vonda, if we can help it."

"We *can't* help it," Josh said. "Did you forget about the city blowing up? We need Allen today. We've got to prevent mass destruction!"

"Shhh! I haven't forgotten, believe me," said Robbie. "Now, c'mon, before Vonda gets suspicious."

They trooped back into the kitchen just as

Vonda laid plates on the table. "You guys have exactly forty minutes to eat and get dressed. We're leaving precisely at nine-thirty."

"Where are we going?" Allen asked, his eyes alight with curiosity.

"We," and Vonda pointed to Robbie, Josh, and herself, "are going to Sea World."

Allen looked confused. "You're traveling to a water planet?"

"Not quite, Allen," Robbie said quickly. "Sea World is like the zoo, but the animals there all live in water." She turned to Vonda. "Can Allen come?"

"I guess so, if it's okay with his dad."

"I know he'd say yes," Allen assured her. Then he frowned. "But this sounds like one of those activities that needs a ticket."

"Don't worry," Vonda told him. "It's on my mom." Noting Robbie's expression, she added, "She gets discount tickets at work, okay?"

Robbie smiled. "Okay."

Allen caught Vonda's eye and winked knowingly. "So your mom's fighting the ticket-line conspiracy? Excellent."

Both Robbie and Vonda turned bewildered expressions on Allen as Josh snickered and began wolfing down his pancakes.

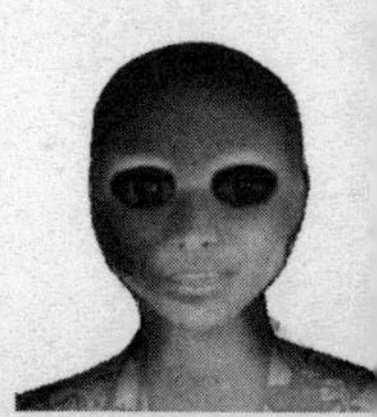

10:13 A.M.
SEA WORLD

For the first time since arriving in San Diego, Allen didn't have to ride in the trunk of a car. Following Josh's example, he hopped into the back seat of Vonda's convertible, and they went roaring down the freeway—until Robbie's face went pale and Vonda slowed down.

Robbie had no idea what they should do about the bay signal problem. Still unsure if there was anything they *could* do about it, she had told Josh and Allen to just enjoy Sea World. They could talk about the signal later. Their main concern now was to keep Vonda from suspecting anything.

So they spent the first hour at Sea World simply trying to keep up with Allen, who was enthralled by all the strange Earth sea life that, up until then, he'd seen only in pictures. "That's a jellyfish?" he said, his nose and hands pressed up against the thick glass wall that separated a huge underwater tank from the air-breathing spectators outside. Big, bulbous, gelatinous creatures with long tendrils gracefully undulated through the water. "Is that where jelly comes from?"

"No way!" Josh said. "Eww, if it did, I'd never eat a peanut butter and jelly sandwich again."

When Allen saw the penguins, he said, "Hey, birds in tuxedos!"

"Those are penguins, and they're not wearing tuxedos," Robbie explained. "They just look as if they are."

Vonda had no idea how close to the truth she came when she pulled Robbie aside and asked, "Is that guy from another planet or what?"

Robbie tried not to look amused as she answered truthfully, "Another planet."

Vonda sighed. "As Josh would say, har-har."

Later, however, Vonda came close to believing that Robbie might have spoken the truth. At the dolphin show, whenever Allen got splashed with water, he closed his eyes and appeared to savor the moment while everybody else squealed in shock. Then, when he got a chance to pet Shamu the killer whale, star of Sea World, he gently laid his hand on the huge sea mammal's snout and grew absolutely still. The strange thing was, so did Shamu. A moment later, Allen burst out laughing. "What's so funny?" Vonda asked him, mystified by this behavior.

"He told me a joke," said Allen. "What did the baby tuna fish say when the hungry shark went after him?"

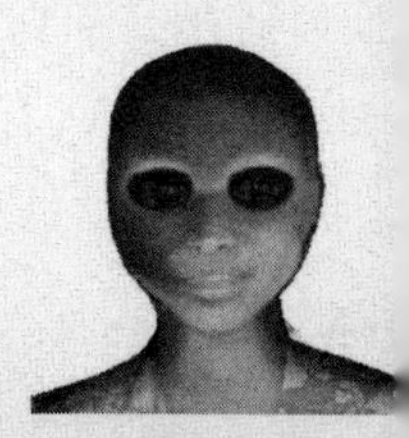

Vonda had no idea.

"Kelp, kelp!"

Robbie and Josh giggled, but Vonda thought they were teasing her. "Right," she said in a sour voice.

"Oh, don't get mad," said Robbie. "Allen's just clowning around."

The highlight of the visit came when Allen got his first look at a tank containing several long electric eels. "Now, these guys I've seen before," he stated. "Well, sort of. They look like Diphidian shock fish, only these are way smaller."

"Diphidian shock fish?" Vonda asked slowly.

Allen nodded. "They live in the turbulent waters of Diphid III's southern ocean. They absorb all the electrical energy around them, store it in their bodies and, when they need to, release it as a defense against enemies."

"Like living lightning guns!" said Josh in awe.

"Exactly," agreed Allen. Then he stopped cold. "Wait a minute . . . absorb energy . . . store it . . . release it at will . . ." He grabbed Robbie's arm. "Robbie, Josh, I have to talk to you. Now!"

"What about me?" Vonda called as they left her in the crowd of eel watchers.

"Don't let anybody get electrocuted," Josh advised her.

When they were safely out of Vonda's hearing range, Robbie gently pulled her arm out of Allen's grasp. "Do you mind telling me what this is all about?"

"I don't mind at all," said Allen. "I've come up with a plan to stop the torpedoes from exploding." He had their full attention now. "All I have to do is go down to the torpedoes themselves, absorb into my own body all of the electrical energy that's accumulated around them, go somewhere safe, and then release it."

"You mean," said Josh, "you could absorb that energy like a battery, and then drain it off, just like that?" and he snapped his fingers.

"Not quite like that," Allen said, snapping his fingers also. "It could be dangerous. For one thing, I don't know exactly how much energy I'd have to absorb, and I have no idea how long I could keep it contained. We Xelans usually generate our own energy; we don't soak it up from other sources."

"Then there's the question of where you'd release it," Robbie said.

"Actually, that's not the problem," Allen told her. "I can direct it harmlessly up into space. The problem is, everybody for miles around will be able to see it."

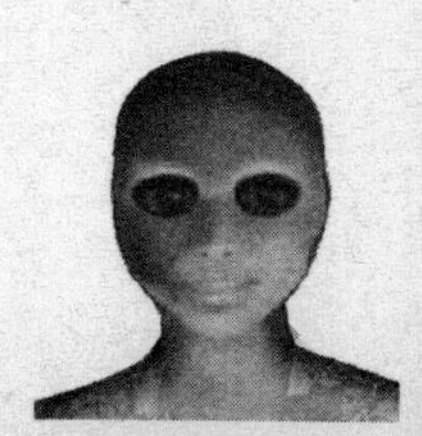

Like a lightning bolt, a brilliant idea hit Robbie. Her eyes sparkled as she suggested, "You mean, it'll look like fireworks?"

The three kids grinned at each other. "Yeah!" they chorused.

5:44 P.M.
THE BURKES' HOUSE

The rest of the day passed quickly, with Robbie, Josh, and Allen in high spirits. Vonda couldn't figure out what had happened between them, but one thing was for sure: they were happy about something. It irked her to be left out, but Robbie finally told her it was something to do with that school assignment Allen had given her the day before. That made Vonda feel better. If it had to do with school, she preferred to be left out.

They finished romping around Sea World and arrived home just as the phone rang. Vonda unlocked the door and flew into the living room to answer it. "Hello?"

Robbie entered to see Vonda's smile fade as the girl listened to the voice on the other end of the telephone line. Then she slammed the receiver back into its cradle and stomped out of the room.

Before Robbie could think what to say, the

phone rang again. It kept on ringing. Obviously Vonda wasn't going to answer it, so Robbie picked it up. "Hello? This is the Burkes' residence."

"Robbie? It's Mom," came Gail's voice.

"Mom? Did you just call?"

"No, Pam did. Is Vonda okay?"

"I don't know. She just hung up and walked out. What's going on?"

"Pam wants to stay after the conference tonight to meet with some colleagues," Gail said. "I told her that our promise to you kids was more important, but she insists this is more important." Gail sounded worried. "I'm going to talk to her, okay, Robbie? Please tell Vonda we'll be there as soon as we can, even if I have to drag Pam away."

Fighting to quell her alarm, Robbie said, "Okay, Mom," and hung up the phone just as Josh walked in.

"What's up?" Josh asked.

"Trouble. Vonda's mom wants to stay late at the conference. Josh, if we can't get to the bay, Allen can't stop the torpedoes."

Vonda appeared in the doorway, her face set in a stern frown. "So much for your advice, Robbie. I knew it sounded too easy to work. Why should

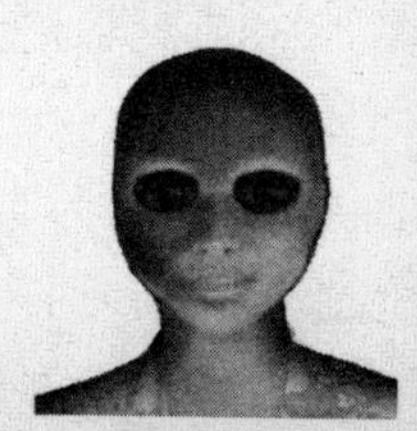

I bother trying to patch up my relationship with my mother? I don't *have* a relationship with her anymore! Your mother loves you, but mine . . ." Tears rolled down her cheeks.

"I'm sorry," Robbie said softly. "Look, my mom said she'll try to talk your mom out of staying after the conference."

"Who cares?" snapped Vonda. "We don't need our mothers. We're going to see the fireworks tonight, and that's that!"

CHAPTER 12

5:56 P.M.
THE BURKES' HOUSE

Grabbing up her keys, Vonda ordered everybody to the car.

Robbie's first thought was to talk Vonda out of going, but she fought the impulse down. This was her only chance to get Allen to the bay at a time when he could absorb and then discharge the torpedo energy without attracting the attention of the entire city. No matter how immature Vonda was acting, no matter how reckless Allen's plan might be, they had to make this trip—the city's safety depended on it.

"Wait," Josh said, suddenly pulling Robbie

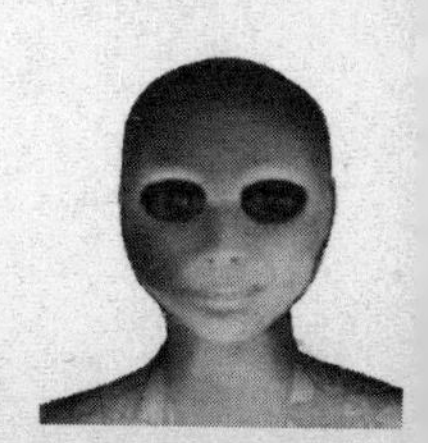

aside. "Allen can't come with us—not like a regular friend, I mean. He'll have to leave the boat when we're out on the water, so Vonda can't know he's there in the first place."

"My gosh, you're right!" Robbie turned to Vonda. "Can we take Allen home first?"

Vonda had forgotten about Allen, and at the moment, she was in no mood to do anybody any favors. "I'll drop him off at the Ferry Landing Marketplace. He can take the ferry back to the convention center." To Allen she said, "That's where your dad is, right?"

Allen had no idea what she was talking about.

"Uh . . . that's right," Robbie blurted, barely remembering the explanation she'd made up the day before. "Okay with you, Allen?"

The alien boy was getting better at picking up cues in situations like this. A spark of understanding lit in his eyes and he said, "Perfect!"

Robbie heaved an inward sigh of relief.

They piled into the car, but before Vonda started the engine, she said in a low voice, "Robbie, I'm sorry I snapped at you before . . . and thanks for agreeing to come along with me. I thought for sure you would try to stop me."

Robbie gulped, not looking forward to the ordeal ahead. "Hey, it's the Fourth of July. It's our right as Americans to see some fireworks, right?"

Vonda nodded. "Right. Let's go!" Vonda slammed the pedal the floor, and the convertible tore off down the road.

Robbie managed to calm Vonda back down to the speed limit, but they still made it to the Ferry Landing Marketplace in record time. "Good-bye, Allen," Vonda said as the alien boy got out of the car. "It was nice meeting you."

"It was a pleasure meeting you too," said Allen. "Bye, everybody!"

The second Vonda's attention was fixed on putting the car back in gear, Allen swiftly turned into his light body and phased into the convertible's trunk. His light particles were barely all the way in when Vonda hit the gas again.

The marina was on Glorietta Bay at the south end of Coronado Island. When they arrived, the docks and beaches were already filled with people who had been watching the annual demonstration show that the Navy SEALs put on for the public every Fourth of July. The air was filled with the sound of happy voices and music, and with the tantalizing scent of hot dogs, fried chicken, and tons of junk food. "Our boat's at the far end," Vonda said, "but I don't think Frank will let me take it out alone."

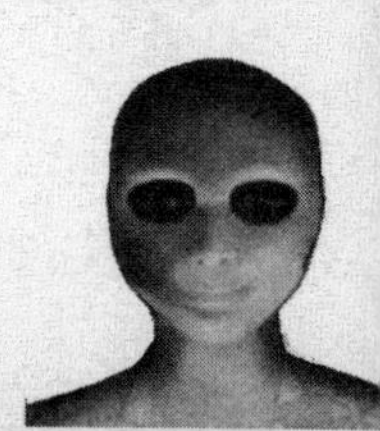

"Who's Frank?" asked Josh.

"He runs the marina." Vonda thought for a moment. "Just follow me and let me do the talking."

Robbie and Josh followed Vonda to the neat little shack that was Frank's office. Frank, a short, squat, happy-looking fellow, beamed with pleasure when Vonda entered. "Why, if it ain't Vonda Burkes. Happy Fourth! Here to enjoy the fireworks, are ya?"

"You bet," Vonda said, "only there's something wrong with our boat and we can't take it out. My mom asked me to rent a boat. You got one?"

Not suspecting a thing, Frank said, "Oh, I think I can find ya somethin'."

Robbie just listened as Vonda glibly lied her way through the transaction, paying with her credit card and assuring Frank that her mother would be coming along any minute. Her heart pounded and her conscience screamed, but Robbie struggled to stay calm and act casual. "We've got to get Allen out on the water," she kept mumbling to herself. "We've got to get Allen out on the water."

The next thing she knew, they were standing before a rental motorboat and Vonda was jingling the keys. "Frank doesn't suspect a thing. That's one of the nice things about being a regular here. We're set!"

"Then let's go," Robbie said, eager to get it all over with.

"Not so fast," said Vonda. "The sun hasn't even set. I'll go to the burger joint over there and get us some dinner. We can eat on the bay, and by the time we're done, it'll be dark. Showtime!" She ran off before Robbie could say another word.

Josh gave his sister a meaningful look. "We're in deep, Robbie."

"Deeper than deep, Josh. I just hope this works."

Allen was standing to Robbie's left, but he'd made his light body invisible. Seemingly out of thin air, his voice asked, "What if your mom and Vonda's mom find out you guys are here?"

Robbie had an answer, but she didn't want to say it. Josh did it for her. "We'll be dead. But if you get those torpedoes drained, it'll be worth it . . . I hope."

7:15 P.M.
THE BURKES' HOUSE

"Vonda! Robbie! Josh! We're home! We're late, but we can still make it to the fireworks!" Gail would have preferred that Pamela call for the

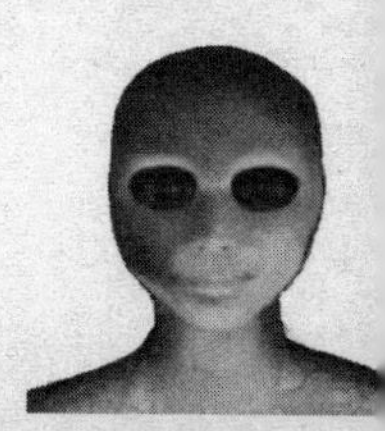

kids, but Pamela was being unusually quiet. It had taken all of Gail's persuasive skills to get her away from the conference. Now Gail wasn't sure if Pamela was angry with her or not.

Both mothers stood quietly at the threshold of the house, listening to silence. "Vonda? Robbie?" Gail tried again.

Her jaw set, her lips pursed, Pamela strode into the living room. Spying a piece of paper taped to the TV, she snatched it up and read aloud, "Gone to fireworks. Robbie." Pamela whirled on Gail. "They went off by themselves!"

"Now, calm down, PeeBee," Gail said, trying to calm her own rising anxiety. "I'm sure there's a reasonable explanation for this."

"Of course there is," Pamela fumed, crushing the note in her fist and throwing the wad of paper on the floor. "I said no, and Vonda disobeyed! I've *had* it with her! No matter how much space I give her, she takes more!" Hooking her purse strap over her shoulder, she headed for the door. "Well, this is the last straw."

Pamela already had the car started by the time Gail locked the door and sat down in the passenger seat. "PeeBee, please, calm down a minute—"

"Gail, you don't understand." Pamela clutched

the steering wheel so hard her knuckles turned white. "You and Robbie have a wonderful relationship, but Vonda and I have drifted apart. I don't know how it happened. I don't know what to do anymore."

"First things first," Gail said. Gently she reached over to the car keys and turned the ignition off. The engine died

Pamela didn't protest. She didn't even move. "It's my fault, isn't it? Dan and I split up, and I can't make it as a single mom."

"I can't answer that," Gail said truthfully. "But what matters, Pam, is that you care about Vonda. And she cares about you, believe me. All you two need is time."

"Which is exactly what I'm not giving Vonda." Pamela sniffed. Tears formed in her eyes. "I've really blown it, haven't I?"

"No, you haven't," Gail assured her. "Even moms get a second chance. Maybe all this is Vonda's way of telling you that." Trying to lighten the moment, Gail added, "Robbie, on the other hand, has some explaining to do."

Pamela gave a weak little chuckle. "Well, at least they can't do anything foolish. Frank—the man who's in charge of the marina—won't let them take the boat out alone."

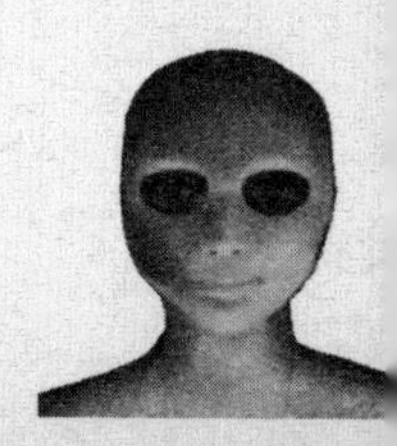

"Good. Then let's go get them. We can patch things up . . . maybe even enjoy some of the fireworks." Gail put her hand on Pamela's shoulder. "It'll be okay, Pam. I know this game. I've played it before. It's no fun, but nobody said that raising kids would be easy."

That made Pamela laugh. "You're right about that." She sniffed again, then pointed at the keys, still dangling from the ignition. "Can I turn the car back on now?"

Gail smiled. "We can't get to the marina otherwise."

8:12 P.M.
GLORIETTA BAY

"This is living!" Vonda stretched out on the padded seat and popped the last bit of hamburger into her mouth. The sun had just set, and a frisky breeze had begun to blow—not cold but just brisk enough to relieve the heavy heat of a summer's day. "I wish I could live out here and just float my life away," Vonda sighed.

"It is beautiful," Robbie agreed, snacking on french fries. For every fry she ate, she passed one on to Josh, who nonchalantly dropped it down into the waiting hand of a certain alien who happened to be hiding under a tarp.

In the small motorboat they'd rented, it had taken no time at all to reach the middle of the bay. Vonda had cut the motor and they'd started eating. Lots of boats were drifting on the placid water, filled with people celebrating the Fourth in their own special seafaring way. Music and voices from every direction carried across the water, but nobody minded the odd mix of sounds. One thing had brought them all together—Independence Day, a holiday when Americans celebrated their right to life, liberty, and the pursuit of happiness. That was exactly what they were all doing now—pursuing happiness. The one happy event that had brought them together this evening was the fireworks display, which would start within half an hour.

As twilight settled in, a hand reached out from under the tarp and poked Robbie's ankle. Robbie took the signal. "Hey, Vonda, what's down that way?" she asked, and pointed at nothing in particular on the shore.

Vonda turned to look, and from the corner of her eye, Robbie saw the tarp rustle. A lithe dark form slipped out from under it, silently dropped over the gunwales of the boat, and disappeared into the water. "Be careful, Allen," Robbie murmured.

As Vonda began to explain the line of buildings that Robbie had pointed to, Robbie and Josh exchanged a knowing glance. There were going to be fireworks on display tonight, no doubt about it. There would be more fireworks than anyone could possibly imagine.

8:16 P.M.
THE MARINA

Pamela had assured Gail that the kids couldn't get out onto the water alone, and now they stood in front of the proof: Pamela's boat was bobbing at its dock, moored as securely as ever. "They're probably in one of the restaurants," she told Gail.

"Hey, what are you doing here?" came a voice.

The women turned to see a short man coming down the dock toward them. In the dim twilight, Gail couldn't see his features, but Pamela knew him. "Frank!" she called.

"I came by to see what was wrong with your boat," Frank said, "but there ain't nothing wrong with it that I can see."

Pamela tensed. "What do you mean?"

Frank was close enough now that Gail could see his eyes go wide. "Vonda . . . she rented a boat in your name, said something was wrong with yours. The rental's not here, so I figured you and she . . ." He trailed off, realizing that he'd made a terrible mistake.

Gail held Pamela's arm gently but firmly. "Don't panic," she said. "We'll find them."

8:27 P.M.
UNDERWATER IN GLORIETTA BAY

Allen had never been so deep below Earth waters before. The experience was wonderfully pleasant. In his natural Xelan light body, he could dart through the current faster than any fish, the glow of his own body lighting his path for him.

As he glided along, marveling at how beautiful the underwater world was, he came face-to-face with a variety of curious fish, many of whom tried to eat his light particles, thinking they might be some new species of tasty insect. The fishy nibblings tickled, and Allen had to shoo the fish away in order to move forward.

Glorietta Bay was just a small inlet of the much larger San Diego Bay. Swimming as fast as he could, Allen left Vonda's motorboat far behind, following the signal that he'd first detected, a signal he could sense much more

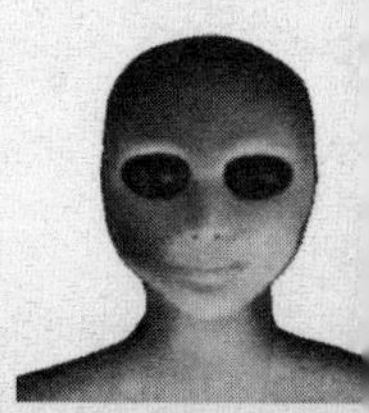

clearly now. Zeroing in on the exact coordinates of the echo was another matter, however. Concentrating hard, he utilized all of his natural homing abilities to pinpoint the exact location. He didn't have much time—he had to find those buried torpedoes and absorb their energy before the fireworks show began.

A distant whistling noise reached his ears, followed by a muffled boom. The fireworks show! It had started already! Allen picked up speed, zooming through a thick school of little silvery bodies that parted like a zipper to allow him through, then closed up behind him as if nothing had happened. He swerved around rocks and parted clumps of seaweed like a knife. The echoing signal grew louder, and Allen descended farther, down, down, down, until he reached the bottom of the bay.

Holding out his light hands, he used his alien energy to create a whirling current above the sand. The suction drew up sand, dirt, and debris until a hole appeared and grew deeper and deeper. From this far down Allen could barely hear the boom of fireworks above the water's surface, but he could feel every vibration as the rockets were launched and as they exploded high in the sky.

He was running out of time.

There! Through the flying sand he could see a group of rounded humps in the harbor floor. Five decades underwater had rotted away their wooden crates and buried the torpedoes under a thick layer of silt, but he could clearly see their metal forms. Allen plunged his light arms into the mud until he touched the torpedoes themselves. Then, concentrating, he drew their electrical energy into himself as fast as he dared.

The sensation was startling. For the first time in his young life, Allen had an idea what it was like to be on the receiving end of a Xelan power burst. Every light particle of his body quivered. He felt giddy, and his senses grew supersharp, almost too sharp. Sight and sound began to hurt. His hands shook and he felt dizzy.

Too late he realized that he didn't have enough time to swim to the fireworks site and release the energy there, as he'd planned. There was too much energy, and it was too strong. He zipped through the water as fast as he could, trying to stick to the plan, but he knew he'd never make it.

CHAPTER 13

8:32 P.M.
GLORIETTA BAY

Despite the harrowing adventure occurring far beneath the surface of the water, Robbie and Josh couldn't help staring at the fireworks. The entire sky was ablaze with multicolored lights, flashing and sparkling, sizzling and roaring as they exploded through the heavens, as brilliant as stars for a few brief seconds, then gone forever. The crowd roared its approval as each display scattered light in every direction. Waves of applause rolled across the water.

Suddenly the water grew turbulent. Boats rocked, and Robbie wondered if an earthquake was shaking the city. She grasped for a handhold as Josh cried out, "The water! Look at the water!"

Sparks of light were dancing across the surface of the bay. At first Robbie thought it was beautiful. Then she realized it was electrical energy. The motors of boats all around her sparked, and the motor of their own boat suddenly burst into flame.

Acting quickly, she grabbed up the two nearest fire extinguishers. "Activate this!" she yelled, tossing one to Josh and aiming a stream of foam at the fire with the other. "Smother the flames!" With Josh and Vonda's help, they put the fire out just in time to see a streak of blinding white light burst out of the water to the east, at the mouth of the bay. People gasped and yelled as the rocket of light shot upward and exploded, scattering silver sparkles for miles around.

Vonda gawked up at it, her jaw slack. "Whoa . . ." she murmured, impressed and startled at the same time.

Robbie and Josh exchanged glances. There was no doubt about it: that had to be Allen. Something had gone wrong, but what? And was Allen all right?

"Vonda!" yelled a voice across the water.

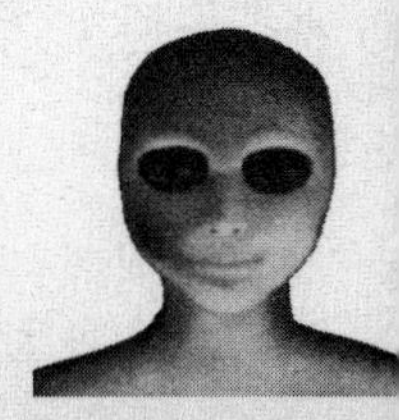

Vonda turned. *"Mom?"*

A rental boat was speeding toward them. "Vonda Burkes, are you all right?" This voice belonged to Frank. With him were Gail and Pamela. As the fireworks show continued to blaze above them, Frank's boat eased up to Vonda's. "We saw fire! You kids okay?"

"The fire's out! We're okay!" Robbie yelled above the din of overhead explosions.

"Fine now, doomed later," Josh said in her ear.

He was right, Robbie knew. They were in for the lecture of a lifetime, and they'd both probably be grounded for all eternity, but that didn't matter to her right now. All she cared about now was Allen. Where was he? Was he okay?

She got her answer when Josh tugged on her sleeve. "Robbie!" He pointed to a boat floating some distance away.

The occupants of the boat were easy to see. They'd turned on nearly every light on their vessel, and they were gabbling in excitement as they hauled a young boy up out of the water. "M'gosh, son, did you fall overboard?" Robbie heard a man ask. She could see Allen, wet and weak, nod his head.

Grinning with relief, Robbie waved over at him. Allen saw her and waved back. "He's okay," she said to Josh. "It must have worked after all."

"Good," said Josh, "because we've got our hands full of angry mothers now."

10:20 P.M.
THE BURKES' HOUSE

Robbie, Josh, and Vonda stood in the center of the living room as Gail and Pamela read them the riot act. The kids stood quietly, letting their mothers vent the fear and frustration that had plagued them ever since they'd come home and found Robbie's note. For once, Robbie kept her mouth shut, knowing that she deserved every harsh word that flew at her. What she'd done had been really stupid. Necessary, but stupid. Her only regret was that she couldn't tell her mother the real reason for it all.

The lecturing stopped when Vonda began to cry. At first, Robbie thought Vonda was just being a baby, and she expected Pamela to get even angrier. Instead, both mothers fell silent. Then, unexpectedly, Pamela rushed over to her daughter and hugged her tight. "I'm sorry," said Pamela. "I'm sorry, honey. What you did tonight was foolish, but what I've been doing to you is even worse."

"I'm sorry, Mom," Vonda sobbed. "I love you."

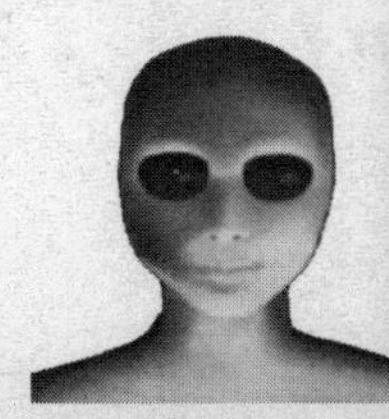

Gail silently gestured Robbie and Josh to her side. "Let's leave them alone."

They went into the kitchen and sat down at the table. "I'm sorry too, Mom," Robbie finally said.

"Me too," said Josh.

Gail could only shake her head. "I don't know what was going through your minds tonight, but obviously you two need to clean up your act. Big time. I'm going to talk to your father about this."

Robbie blanched. "Oh, do you have to?"

Gail just glared at her.

"Yes, you have to," Robbie answered herself.

"But before I do, I need to ask you something." Gail hesitated, as if she didn't want to say the next words. "Have I been ignoring you kids in favor of my work?"

Both Robbie and Josh were about to say, "No, of course not," but Gail went on before they could say it.

"I mean, sometimes I think I'm the one who broke up the family, just because I wanted a career. Did . . . did I do that?"

"Mom," said Robbie, "you're allowed to want a career just as much as Dad's allowed to want his. If there'd been a great hospital job available in Delport, you would have taken it, right?"

"You bet," Gail assured her.

"Well, there you are."

When Gail visibly relaxed, Robbie felt her heart swell up with pride. As much as she hated her family's situation, she knew it wasn't anybody's fault. It pleased her to be able to make her mom feel better about the whole unfortunate mess. "You know what Josh always says," she added.

Gail and Josh both said, "What's that?" at the same time.

"Reality bites."

Gail laughed. "Yeah, sometimes it does, doesn't it?" She reached out and grasped her children's hands. "But it has its rewards. I wouldn't trade the two of you for anything in or out of this world."

"Does that mean you won't tell Dad about tonight?" Josh asked hopefully.

"Good try, but no," Gail replied. "I'm afraid this is one reality bite you're going to have to swallow."

Robbie turned to Josh and sighed. "Well, we might as well enjoy our last night of freedom," she advised him. "Dad's gonna ground us forever."

Josh just gave her a pouty look. "So I *was* right. Reality bites."

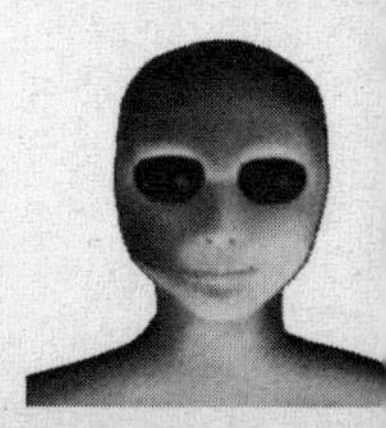

Robbie and Josh were ordered straight to bed. They'd have to get up early to catch the morning train. But before lights out, Robbie sneaked into the den to find Allen there with Josh. "So what happened?" she asked Allen, bursting with curiosity.

"I nearly overloaded," Allen explained. "I tried to make it to the fireworks site, but I couldn't."

"You sure gave everybody a shock," Josh told him, "literally. Our motor caught on fire."

"Sorry about that," said Allen. "Like I said, I almost overloaded myself. Some of the energy sort of leaked out, and you know that water and electricity don't mix."

"The explosion in the sky—was that *you?*" Robbie asked.

Allen grinned as if proud of a particularly clever magic trick. "Yup. I knew the outflow of energy was too great for me to control, so I let it take me up with it. I couldn't release it without losing my own form."

"You blew up?" Josh asked in awe.

"Sort of. But, as you would say, it was a rush."

The kids laughed, then they all automatically clapped their hands over their mouths. "Shhh!" Robbie whispered. "We'd better get to bed, or we'll end up in even more trouble. G'night, Josh.

G'night, Allen." She headed for the door. "Oh, and Allen—thanks."

As always, Allen gave her that wide smile of his that made everything okay. "You're welcome," he said cheerfully.

When Robbie tiptoed into Vonda's room and her head hit the pillow, she couldn't help but grin. What a vacation! She'd helped save a mother-daughter relationship and a city, all in two days. "Independence," she murmured. It could be pretty fun as well as pretty scary.

She couldn't wait for her eighteenth birthday.

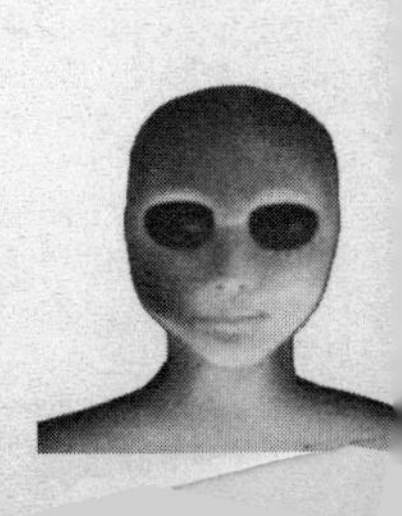

Alien Fact File

Gronolopolis

Location: A hundred Zutrons, or approx. 7 million light-years away from Xela.

Inhabitants: The Gronpoly is a round creature with three floppy ears, a big mouth, and an even bigger appetite. It is actually composed of two animals, the Gron and the Poly.

Characteristics: The Gron is the thinker of the two halves. The Poly is the reactor of the two halves. Gronpolies have excellent hearing. They adore their ears. "All life is radio."

Info about the symbiotic relationship of Grons and Polys: The two need each other to survive. The thinker can't do anything without the reactor. Thinking is the equivalent of eating, so the thinker needs the reactor to do that.

Average lifespan: 50 Ilops

Number of Gronpolies on Gronolopolis: Too many to count. Closest estimate is 6 billion, but Gronpolies reproduce constantly at exponential rates. The planet is extremely overpopulated.

Number of Gronpolies on Earth: Gronpolies, like most aliens, don't care for Earth.

Scientific Advances: Gronpoly spaceships are hard and round and can roll for miles on hard terrain. However, Gronpolies are not good navigators and often get lost in distant galaxies.

Biggest fear: Black holes

Interesting fact: Laughing will loosen up a Gronpoly's digestive system and force whatever he's eaten (usually furniture) out of his stomach in a giant burp. Showing him human TV soap operas is a good method for making a Gronpoly laugh.

Arc Alien File reference #: 0835

Josh Stevenson's Alien File #: 005

About the Authors

Bobbi JG Weiss and David Cody Weiss have never met Allen Strange personally, but they have encountered a few Trykloids. For this reason, they own five fearsome watchcats that guard their home, plus several fish that are trained to splash real loud in their aquariums if a Trykloid should ever break down the door. They also have many houseplants that have been genetically modified to jump out of their pots and attack hostile aliens on sight.

When they're not battling Trykloids, Bobbi and David write for a living. Among their credits are *The Journey of Allen Strange: The Arrival*; six *Sabrina the Teenage Witch* novels; two upcoming *Sabrina* titles; three *Star Trek: Starfleet Academy* novels; a *Secret World of Alex Mack* novel; and four *Are You Afraid of the Dark?* novels. They have also written animation, trading cards, CD-ROMs, film scripts, and other stuff.

Like Phil Berg, Bobbi and David dream of being abducted by aliens one day, but only if those aliens are friendly and give them lots of chocolate to eat.

NICKELODEON/MINSTREL BOOKS POINTS PROGRAM

Official Rules

1. *HOW TO COLLECT POINTS*

Points may be collected by purchasing any book with the special Minstrel®/Nickelodeon "Read Books, Earn Points, Get Stuff!" offer. Only books that bear the burst "Read Books, Earn Points, Get Stuff!" are eligible for the program. Points can be redeemed for merchandise by completing the coupons (found in the back of the books) and mailing with a check or money order in the exact amount to cover postage and handling to Minstrel Books/Nickelodeon Points Program, P.O. Box 7777-G140, Mt. Prospect, IL 60056-7777. Each coupon is worth points. (See individual book for point value.) Copies of coupons are not valid. Simon & Schuster is not responsible for lost, late, illegible, incomplete, stolen, postage-due, or misdirected mail.

2. *40 POINT MINIMUM*

Each redemption request must contain a minimum of 40 points in order to redeem for merchandise.

3. *ELIGIBILITY*

Open to legal residents of the United States (excluding Puerto Rico) and Canada (excluding Quebec) only. Void where taxed, licensed, restricted, or prohibited by law. Redemption requests from groups, clubs, or organizations will not be honored.

4. *DELIVERY*

Allow 6-8 weeks for delivery of merchandise.

5. *MERCHANDISE*

All merchandise is subject to availability and may be replaced with an item of merchandise of equal or greater value at the sole discretion of Simon & Schuster.

6. *ORDER DEADLINE*

All redemption requests must be received by January 31, 2000, or while supplies last. Offer may not be combined with any other promotional offer from Simon & Schuster. Employees and the immediate family members of such employees of Simon & Schuster, its parent company, subsidiaries, divisions and related companies and their respective agencies and agents are ineligible to participate.

COMPLETE THE COUPON AND MAIL TO
NICKELODEON/MINSTREL POINTS PROGRAM
P.O. BOX 7777-G140
MT. PROSPECT, IL 60056-7777

NICKELODEON®
MINSTREL® BOOKS

NAME ______________________________

ADDRESS ______________________________

CITY ______________________________ STATE _____ ZIP ______

THIS COUPON WORTH FIVE POINTS
Offer expires January 31, 2000

I have enclosed _____coupons and a check/money order (in U.S. currency only) made payable to "Nickelodeon/Minstrel Books Points Program" to cover postage and handling.

❑ 40–75 points (+ $3.50 postage and handling)
❑ 80 points or more (+ $5.50 postage and handling)

1464-02(2of2)

FULL HOUSE™ SISTERS

A brand-new series starring Stephanie AND Michelle!

#1 Two On The Town

Stephanie and Michelle find themselves
in the big city—and in big trouble!

#2 One Boss Too Many

Stephanie and Michelle think camp will be major fun.
If only these two sisters were getting along!

When sisters get together...expect the unexpected!